HOLLOW WORLD

ESCAPE FROM LIMBO

PART I

Lukos has served Sir Patterwicke Doyle and his estate for most of his life. It's custom for a boy, on his nineteenth birthday, to leave his life of servitude and venture into a new life of his own.

And so, Lukos leaves behind a life of obscurity to take his place in the world. Except, Lukos was never meant to leave . . .

And now, all Hell has been released to find him.

Lukos very quickly realizes that Doyle, and the other nobles, are willing to stop at nothing to bring him back home.

But why? What could they possibly want with a lowly servant?

An uncommon street thief finds her new mark. She can't explain her fascination with Lukos, nor why she chooses to help him, even when the Hollow Men set their sights on her as well. Now she's marked, and all of Limbo is being turned inside out to find them both.

Brought together by a simple act of thievery, the runaway and the pickpocket must play a dangerous game of escape before the Hollows and their masters destroy everything they've built to get to Lukos.

What neither Kit nor Lukos understand, however, is that everything the masters have built, hinges on Lukos.

HOLLOW WORLD

ESCAPE FROM LIMBO
PART I

Hollow World:
Escape from Limbo

Written by C. Michael McGannon

Cover design by www.FlirtationDesigns.com

Interior illustrations by Rainey Leigh (www.facebook.com/Crookerd.spine.art)

Published by Wyvern's Peak Publishing, 2020
An imprint of The McGannon Group, Ltd. Co.

Hollow World: Escape from Limbo / by C. Michael McGannon — 2nd Ed.

Summary: A house servant and a pickpocket find themselves on the run from a city's royalty and their terrible enforcers.

2   4   6   8   1 0   1 2   1 4   1 6   1 8

ISBN-13: 978-0-9861458-8-9

www.WyvernsPeak.com

PART 1

"It is nothing to die. It is frightful not to live."

– Victor Hugo

Prologue: Escape

The room burned in hues of red and bloodier red, the air hot and sticky. A thick stinging incense held the children hostage, who sat motionless, as if drugged. Each had wide, frenzied eyes, but no one dared move. Perhaps they couldn't even if they had wanted to.

A man draped in black robes, with a strange mask reminiscent of a fly's head, led some form of an animal around the boys subdued within his circle, three times, widdershins. Lukos felt his stomach twist and gnarl. He refused to look at the horned beast.

The dream — *or was it a dream? a memory?* — was familiar. He knew its story all too well — not how it ended, though, not yet. But still. When the man ended his ceremonial walk around the children on the floor, Lukos could hear the knife tear into the animal's short-haired pelt. The creature gave a sad, terrified bleat, as a spray of blood flecked Lukos' face.

He woke up shivering in his metal-framed bed. The same one that cut into his back and legs due to the thin and worn mat that pretended to be a mattress. Some of the other servants watched him from their own beds, tired, irritated, or bored. Lukos apologized to no one in particular and rolled out of bed, leaving behind comfortless sheets soaked with sweat, and the memory of his perturbed dreams. He needed a shower, especially today.

His birthday. The day of his release.

Today, he would finally be rid of this place, as anyone who was born into Doyle's service would, at their nineteenth birthday, be given the means to venture out into the wider world and . . .

Lukos wasn't sure what he was going to do with himself, to be honest. He smiled, giddy, already forgetting his recurring nightmare.

After a cold shower—the servant's quarters were not provided hot, or even warm, water—Lukos dressed himself in the finest clothes he owned; the frilled shirt and the nice jacket issued to him for formal dinners and special occasions. His things were packed and ready as he quietly took to the stairs. Not that he had much to pack.

He knocked on the large oak door, which read: *BEGOR*.

"Enter," answered a woman's dispassionate voice.

Lukos stepped inside. Bell Begor stood tall and lean, an imposing woman, as the head of staff should be. Her indigo dress and white collar a stark contrast against a room of yellowed sheaves of parchment, dark wood grains, and gray charcoal sketches. Quill and paper in hand, the prim head of staff raised her head from the crowded desk to glance at Lukos. Her eyes were sharp but distant, seeing straight through Lukos, her mind somewhere else. Somewhere infinitely more important.

"Lukos. What is it?"

"I'm ready, ma'am."

"Ready," Begor repeated slowly, rolling the word around in her mouth like cheap bourbon, an unknowing gaze painted on her face. "Ready for what, Lukos?"

He could hardly keep the smile from his face. "Today's

my nineteenth birthday. I'm ready to accept my apprenticeship elsewhere. Is it in the Arts District, or Business?" Lukos hoped they had not chosen a new master in Industrial for him to live with, though he would still be happy to go.

"Ah." Begor nodded in a wave of nonchalance, her eyes still dead. "I see. Unfortunately, we will still be requiring your services here."

The world became all too quiet, the air heavy like molasses. Lukos felt his heartbeat slow as his mind struggled to understand her words.

"Here, ma'am?" he asked, voice faltering. "But . . . we *all* leave on our nineteenth birthday. After we've served. No one stays past nineteen."

"Perhaps Lord Doyle sees something greater in you and has decided your career should remain within these walls. I do not know."

"That can't be."

Begor turned back to her desk, her tall form bending to hover over her papers. Papers detailing new automatons, blueprints for city buildings, and older designs for Hollow

Men. A dusty old scroll detailed some monstrosity of metal arms—a factory or mining automaton, perhaps. Papers ill-suited for the desk of a head-of-staff.

"May I speak with him?" panic reached for Lukos' voice. He waited, hanging on her response, hoping, praying. Begging for the chance that she might be wrong.

"Speak with Lord Doyle?" A single, mirthless chuckle clipped her words. "I think not. Go now, to the kitchens with you. Get about your chores, Lukos."

"But . . ."

Bell Begor stood up from her work, unfolding to stand straight, towering, her eyes locking with his. Dead eyes. Apathetic on the surface. But something burned behind them that shut him up immediately.

Lukos swallowed, his own gaze clinging to the floor, sulking on his way out. As the door closed behind him, Lukos felt lightheaded. Years of disappointment, anger, abuse, despair—and the promise of *escape*—crashed down on him all at once.

The kitchen was already alive with movement; servants bustling about, preparing food, and carrying sacks of goods. On Lukos' entrance, the other servants looked surprised, as did Chef Burkely. The tall, ebony-skinned man smiled, ever cheerful. "What are you still doing here, boyo? And so well dressed? Come to say goodbye?"

Lukos found no response. A bell rang on the wall. A single, small silver bell amidst rows. Hundreds of them, all labeled. This one was labeled: *Library*.

"Looks like his lordship is up early today." Burkely quickly put breakfast onto a silver tray, filling it with juice and coffee, eggs, toast laden with jam, and blood sausage. The meat was grown by the finest bio-alchemists in Limbo, and the coffee, jam, and juice provided by only the most reputable botanic labs. Lukos saw his chance.

"I'll take it," he said just as Burkely handed it to Josef, one of the younger boys.

"But, Lukos, aren't you—"

"Nineteen years old? Yes. And well more than half of that strangled life spent carrying his food to him, chef. What's one more tray?"

Lukos grabbed the tray from Josef, wordless, and pushed his way out of the room. His mind was far away, feet moving on their own accord down a path Lukos had taken for so many years he could walk it with eyes closed. At the end of that path? A fat noble, with a taste for alcohol and women—impatient and pig-headed and dull—awaited his service.

Lord Doyle was well known in Limbo. He was a war hero, and the creator of the Hollow Men, after all—those vigilant authorities that kept their town safe and civil, running like tightly-wound clockwork. But those inside the Doyle Estate knew Bell Begor was the real mastermind behind the machines. She was the true lord of the manor. Doyle was a slob who enjoyed the money and fame. A slob that made Lukos' skin crawl. He intended to talk to Doyle, reason with him. Lukos could not spend another moment of his life in this estate.

As he made his way toward the library, Lukos heard metal bend and tear. He looked down—the edge of the silver platter was crumpled and ruined where his left hand had tightened into a ball. No doubt, he would hear about that.

Or would he? What was holding him back now? *Escape.*

He cursed to himself at the years wasted here. The anger grew until he realized the silver platter was clattering to the floor. The blood sausage mixed with the coffee and orange juice, staining the wallpaper nicely.

Making his decision, Lukos turned away from the library and ran back to the servant quarters as quietly as he could, avoiding the hallways he knew to be well-traveled and busy.

In his library, Lord Patterwicke Doyle tapped his fingers impatient, finishing off the previous night's remains of cranberry wine. He could still smell the escort's perfume, a heady aroma that mingled well with his intoxicant.

Lily.

Doyle favored the girl. The thought of her — or rather her skill set — gave him a warm smile. She was one of the many girls that Ash provided him, quite adept at giving him more than just a smile.

Doyle's stomach growled, yanking him from the indulgent memories of the night before. He rang the bell again.

The staff was usually more prompt, trained to be efficient under his strong leadership and emphasis on order. He was displeased at having to wait so long. Another minute went by before Doyle snatched a communicator from the wall. "Burkely!" he shouted into the brass cone. "Where is my breakfast?"

He fiddled with the woven metal tube that ran into the wall, waiting for the head chef's answer.

"*Mi'lord?*" came the chef's reply. "*I sent Lukos to you already. He should have well been there by now.*"

Doyle's eyes narrowed. *Lukos. Connor's brat.* If it were any other servant, they would have earned a good lashing for being so late. "Send another to find him, and hurry it along. I don't like it when that boy wanders."

"*Understood, Lord Doyle. My deepest apologies.*"

Lukos hesitated on the threshold of the manor. The handsome, perfectly manicured lawn sprawled before him, and beyond that, the high walls of Doyle's estate. Tips of the

Business District's tallest edifices could be seen, but nothing stood above Oudemonium, the clock tower that stood in the center of the city. It looked down on all of Limbo, the four clock faces watching each district day and night.

Lukos wondered what the consequences of leaving without permission could possibly be, shuddering at remembering dreams of the red room and the dying animal.

Dreams? Memories? Whatever they were.

He laughed at his own preposterousness. He was insignificant. Who would notice if he had slipped off into the morning? And if anyone did notice, Lukos doubted they would care. He'd been forced to stare at Limbo's skyline for the better part of the past two decades, mostly from the inner pane of a window. *And for what?* To give a fat, aging noble his daily meals. Hundreds more were available to do the same thing. It was Lukos' time to see the city for himself, and not from behind glass.

A sense of liberation swelled within his breast as his foot trod upon the first blades of bio-alchemical grass. *No, they don't need me anymore,* Lukos assured himself.

Prologue: Escape

His thinking couldn't have been more wrong.

Bell Begor appeared on the street in front of Oudemonium. No one had noticed her there until a man nearly bumped into her. He blushed, stroking his moustache and lifting his hat in apology in one smooth moment, but the tall woman was already at the tower's riveted doors, disappearing inside.

Inside and up, up, up she went. The lift groaned, seeming to move beyond its normal speed, as if her urgency made the machine nervous. Bell stepped out at the top floor, her terse footsteps over the marble floor muted by hisses of steam and the grating cacophony of gears. All around the tower, behind each face and suspended above her head, the giant clockwork carried out its labor, tired and worn after its lonely decades of existence. From behind the tower's four clock faces one could see all of Limbo laid out in a sprawling circle below, the city itself like a giant clock.

Bell ignored all but the black cylinder in the center of the tower—a circular room enclosed from the outside world. Repetitious patterns of words and sigils were etched into the surface. Through the open door, a man sat writing at his desk under a single, dreary light that hung from the room's ceiling. She entered unannounced.

Shekelton O'Toole was a man thin and gaunt. As the archduke of Limbo, his clothes were fine and his white hair well-kempt, but one could see years of stress and history beginning to take its toll. The silver pendant hanging around his neck, as well as the silver ring on his left hand, looked out of place in his otherwise strict attire. Both were flourishing, crafted in the form of snakes. They shone brightly under the light, snake eyes glimmering.

He barely looked up at Bell as she entered the room, pausing to stroke his pendant.

"Miss Begor. To what do I owe the pleasure?" he asked, sounded anything but pleasured.

"Lukos has run away. He is missing."

Shekelton O'Toole's nostrils flared. He set down his quill and massaged his temple, still grasping the pendant with his other hand.

"Why now? Why today, of all days?"

"I cannot answer that, my lord. The timing is inconvenient."

"I wasn't asking you," he snapped. "What of Doyle?"

"He said he would begin a search plan."

"Which means he's done nothing."

A faint buzzing came from outside the room, and O'Toole and Bell Begor both looked to the door as two men joined them.

Both were immaculately dressed. One was crowned with a black top hat and a shiny orange band, offsetting the brown suede coat that complimented his thicker middle. His upbeat attitude accentuated a constant look of amused superiority, or perhaps assessment. The other dressed in a luxurious gray and white suit, filled out with green andradite buttons and cufflinks, gold buckles for his belt and shoes. His thin framed spectacles held circular emerald lenses, so thick they completely hid his eyes. Mr. Zeb and Mammon, O'Toole's attendants and lieutenants, for a lack of better titles.

Any of the three figures before O'Toole were imposing on their own. Together, their presence was overpowering.

"Bell Begor," exclaimed Mr. Zeb. He smiled, chocolate eyes crinkling at the edges. "What brings you all the way to Oudemonium?"

"Lukos is escaping," she explained dispassionately.

Mr. Zeb looked shocked. "*Is* escaping?"

"I want every Hollow Man in Limbo out looking for him," said O'Toole. "I don't care where you have to pull them from, and I don't care how it affects the town. Just find him."

"Now, now." Mr. Zeb crossed the room, walking around the desk to place a reassuring hand on O'Toole's shoulder. An orange-black fly crawled from his shirt sleeve toward O'Toole's jacket. "Don't worry, Shekelton. It is in our best interest to find him."

O'Toole swatted the man's hand away and glared until Mr. Zeb stepped back from behind the desk. "I will leave the matter to you, then. Be quick about it"

Mr. Zeb's smile was approving. He nodded at his companion. "Bell, my dear."

Bell Begor waited, unmoving.

"Go tell Ash we need her to keep her ear to the ground. And Mammon," the other man straightened, colored glasses glinting with anticipation, "get LaCrucis up here. He's good with this sort of thing."

A smirk sent cracks along Mammon's cheeks. He nodded and, with Bell Begor, turned to leave the room.

"No!"

All three servants of the nobles turned to look at O'Toole. A lesser man might have faltered.

"I don't want that thing involved. Lukos would not come back in one piece. I will not have LaCrucis running around my city."

Mr. Zeb's smile slid from his face, but he nodded. "As you wish."

He turned back to Bell and Mammon. "I want all of your Hollow Men tuned to my command. Tell Ash as well."

Bell nodded.

"Are we to wake LaCrucis' Hollow Men?" asked Mammon.

Mr. Zeb looked at O'Toole. "Let them sleep, for now."

As Bell and Mammon left the room, Mr. Zeb turned to Limbo's somber leader. He circled the desk again, standing dangerously close to O'Toole's shoulder.

"You shouldn't fear LaCrucis so. He is our greatest tool."

"It is a monster."

"Yes, but when have you shied away from using monsters?"

"You will bring back Lukos in the manner that I choose, Zeb. Now get out."

Respectful amusement masked Mr. Zeb's face. "Very well, my lord. Trust me to carry out your will."

Chapter One: The Runaway and the Pickpocket

The Doyle Estate was in chaos, and no one knew just why. Hours passed, and Lukos had yet to be seen again. Slipping back into his military days, Lord Doyle had lined up members of his staff, giving commands for the servant boy to be found without delay. When the butler, Pierre, frowned at this, Doyle struck the man and then screamed his orders into the communicator and down the halls for anyone else to hear. Staff from every section of the house stopped their daily duties to look for Lukos, as frightened as they were confused.

As for Patterwicke Doyle himself, he marched back and forth in his study, nervous, waiting—hoping—for one of his house staff to drag the boy in by his shirt. The door opened and Doyle spun, his heart racing . . .

. . . and then his heart went cold. Bell Begor stood in the doorway, her lifeless gaze fixed on him.

"This does not bode well for you."

Doyle drew himself up with an arrogant harrumph. "I don't know what you're talking about."

"Don't pretend! You were given this position for the purpose of guarding Lukos."

"Lukos, as well as the other boys. He is not the only lamb in this flock."

"Very well. And you are not the only noble capable, or available, to do the job." Her eyes narrowed. "Your orders . . . my lord?"

Doyle's fingers fidgeted with the seam of his morning jacket. His earlier bravado melted away. Drink and luxury had made him slow over the years. They both knew her question was simply a formality of contract. "My orders? Find him, of course. I trust your judgment, Bell."

She curtsied, turning mechanically toward the doorway.

"Wait, where are you going? Aren't you going to help?"

"Lukos isn't in your library. He's out there. In Limbo."

Lord Doyle swallowed her words like soured milk. The realization of the exact consequences of Lukos' disappearance hit him hard. He leaned against his high-back chair, the strained wood creaking under his considerable weight, and looked out the window. Bell Begor was already gliding across his sculpted lawn. He lifted the communicator to his lips.

"Pierre."

The butler's voice was cold. "*My lord.*"

"Fetch the steam carriage. I am going out."

Lukos was bombarded with a steady barrage of sensory overload. From the busy roar of the cobbled streets to the watchful peaks of gilded buildings, he took it all in. Squeezing his prized pocket watch for comfort, he made a few steps toward a shop window filled with automaton pets, mesmerized. Doyle, even though he was one of Limbo's richer residents, never indulged in any pets. Lukos was taken with fascination, eyes drinking up every sight the district had to offer.

His movement toward the shop was a mistake. Lukos paid more attention to the way the sun glimmered over the metal body of a rat than the direction he was going. Somebody collided with him, and the timepiece that Lukos had been holding was bludgeoned from his hand. It took him a moment to recover from the shock before he spied it spinning over the cobbles.

"Watch where you're walking!" the man scolded, briskly stomping past. Lukos mumbled an apology, forcing his way into the crowd to chase down his timepiece. He reached out his hand and was promptly kicked in the elbow. A passerby yelled obscenities behind him, not stopping for a proper talking to. Lukos ignored the pain in his arm and grabbed the watch, merely a moment before it rolled over a grate.

With a shaky sigh of relief, he stood and wiped the hunter-casing clean. Its silver back was scuffed, but the front crest — a wolf with wings flying toward the sun — was unmarked. Afraid of losing it for good, Lukos stuffed it back into his front breast pocket.

Lukos looked around, not recognizing any of the buildings. After purposefully getting lost to avoid anyone retrieving him, he had tried to follow the early morning crowd to the Business District, after which he knew he could make his own way to the Industrial District. Getting lost had worked only too well. He had no clue where he was.

"Excuse me," he mumbled. "Excuse me, can you help . . . ?"

The crowd paid him no mind. Lukos scanned his surroundings and saw a vendor on the street corner selling cheap tea. He approached the man and caught his eye, which twinkled above rosy red cheeks.

"Good day, sir. Please, can you point me to the Industrial District?"

The tea vendor's eye lost its twinkle. "I sell tea, not directions. Buy some or go away."

A man behind Lukos made his presence known, checking the time with enough commotion and exaggerated gestures to ensure Lukos was aware of his impatience.

"Fine. I'll take whatever your best tea is." Lukos pulled

out a gold coin and pushed it forward on the vendor's cart, causing the vendor to gasp.

"It's only two pence a cuppa, sir." Lukos noticed a swift change of tone.

"It's not just for the tea. I want to know how to get to the Industrial District."

The vendor moved to pick up the gold coin, but Lukos held his finger on it. They stared each other down for a moment before the man behind Lukos coughed again.

"Why do you want to go there?" asked the vendor.

"I need work and a place to stay."

"You don't look the type . . ." He stopped as Lukos hardened his gaze. The man bent down to retrieve the cheap plastic cup and pour something watery green from a tumbler. "Let's see . . . fastest way . . . Go down this street for three blocks, right up to a gaudy place called the Grundy Theatre. Then take a right and keep on walking. You'll know when you get to the Industrial District. And when you do, don't say that I did not warn you."

Lukos released the gold piece and took the warm cup from the vendor. The man behind shoved past him with a huff. Lukos looked at the cup in his hand and took a sip, his face quickly twisting to match its flavor — or lack thereof. It was nothing like what he had served at Lord Doyle's estate, more dusty water than tea, and the little flavor it did have was not to his liking. He poured it down another grate where the drink — if it could be called such — would be carried through Limbo's aqueducts to be filtered — though no one really knows how well — and recycled.

Lukos took out the pocket watch, his only real possession. *Already midmorning.* Looking up, he took a deep breath and stepped away from the street corner, watching the street signs as he made his way toward the Industrial District once more.

A place to stay for the night and a solid rest were his intentions for the evening. Those were essential before finding work. He could take a day off to explore and find shelter. After all, it was his birthday.

Kit couldn't believe it. She watched from above as a young man took out a gold coin and placed it on the vendor's cart. He might as well have waved it around for everyone to see. Her keen eyes made out the struggle of wills between the tea-cart man and the fresh-faced patron, before the vendor pointed this way and that. *A gold coin . . . for directions?*

She sat forward, trying to see through the crowd as the new owner of a costly cup of tea walked away, nearly falling off of her roof when she saw him spew the tea and pour it down the drain into the underworld below.

She gave his clothes a good one-over. Tailored, expensively made. *Rich*, Kit decided. Spending an entire gold coin on tea. *So he's stupid.* Asking for directions. *Lost.* And then he wasted the tea. *And spoiled.*

Kit grinned. *Jackpot.*

A *click-clack* sound a few rooftops away caught Kit's attention. *Hollow Men.* They must have been on patrol and would be too close, too soon. She marked the rich idiot visually and clambered down the side of the building, using a gray cloak to expertly blend into the daytime shadows of the alleyway. She brushed herself off and straightened her hair, wrapping the cloak around her torso and black leggings, transforming it into a simple dress.

The *click-clack* grew louder still. Without looking, and her heart beating a little faster, Kit rushed forward from the alley and onto the street, matching the speed of the crowd to blend in. As long as no one looked too close, she would remain one of their number—invisible.

Kit switched directions to move behind an older woman crossing the street. Not too close, but close enough that she might pass as the woman's granddaughter. Kit checked the street sign. It was the same that her mark had been walking toward. She picked up her pace. They were on the border between the Arts District and the Residential District—a bit of a no-no for a pickpocket, but business wasn't so good in Industrial these days, and she had to go where the business was. Besides, lesser thieves may get caught here, but not Kit. The fact that getting caught meant getting dead might've had something to do with it.

Another Hollow Man came into view ahead, but this wasn't one of the spider types. This time it was one of those hulking, slow automatons that only patrolled the streets, steam hissing from its clicking joints as it lumbered past. People gave it a wide berth, and Kit quickly let her hair down to hide her face. She looked to cross the street, but there, on the corner opposite of the looming street walker, was a second Hollow Man of the same make. Both Hollows seemed to be watching the small humans bellow, scanning the crowd.

Kit was beginning to panic. *Three Hollow Men within two blocks?* And they were looking for someone. Something was off.

They were blocking her way to some valuable coinage, and more importantly, her way out. She couldn't stay in the Art District for long. The streets would thin and people would start to notice the shabbiness of her clothing, the way her hair wasn't a consistent shade of black, and then . . . suspicion. Then would come the Hollows.

Quickly, she scanned the alleys, trying to find one that was discreet and easy to slip into. She watched—surprised, confused—as the well-to-do she'd been tailing turned into one of those alleyways. She cut the corner, quick-step, following him.

Posters for small one-act street troupes and sleazy-eyed magicians barely clung to the sides of the buildings. Grimy, dank air settled deep in her lungs. Kit didn't like being in this position. *Girl's gotta do what a . . .*

She glimpsed her target rounding a left corner and ran to catch up before he turned again. Finally, she spotted him again in the diminishing crowd. He was already back on the street, peering over his shoulder at the Hollow Men behind them.

Kit frowned. *What are you worried for? Hollows want nothing to do with goody-goodies like you.*

Her curiosity for his destination was reaching to match her desire for his gold. Not quite. *Focus! Keep your eye on the prize, that's what we're here for,* Kit reminded herself. She continued to follow him as they crossed into the Arts District now, where dandies and their friends waltzed the streets in a rich-minded stupor. It was quieter, less crowds during the day, with soft-voiced women and the laid back contemplations of jazz singing from speaker tubes. At night, Arts would become a haven for those in need of entertainment and distraction from the daily grind between

Residential and Business.

Kit seethed at the mental image. *Lucky bastards don't know how well off they are.*

Her mark hung a right on a street corner past some small theater. Kit jogged to keep up. Her mental map recognized the street, and it would be a straight shot back to the Industrial District on this road. Except for maybe having to duck into the shadows here or there, she could make a clean getaway after she'd nicked him. *Am I really this lucky, or is he just that big of a fool?* He was begging her to steal from him.

Another Hollow ambled through the streets like a giant sloth, with its thick stumpy arms and long metal fingers dragging on the ground. Her mark ducked into an art store before the mechanical beast got to him, and that's when she was sure of it. *He's avoiding the Hollows.* Her inner thief was telling her to run, get as far away from this man as she could, that only danger lay ahead.

Pushing her instinct aside, Kit kept walking. Her stomach had stopped growling yesterday, but it still hurt from hunger, and her friends in low places could not afford to keep providing free shelter. She needed this.

She did her best to blend into the back of a group of ritzy dandies and their women out for a splurge on the town, she kept her head low as they passed the Hollow Man. When she was sure the thing had no interest in her, she turned back to make another pass by the art shop.

Her instinct proved right. A bell tinkled as the shop door opened. Out stepped the man she'd been following, who was looking after the Hollow Man. Quite purposefully, she collided with him.

"I-I . . . my apologies!" he stammered, standing there in shock.

For some inexplicable reason, Kit felt frozen looking into his face. It was well-shaped, clean, hopeful, and ignorant of life on the street—the type of face that usually infuriated her.

But right now she was attempting to manage a very different set of emotions. A quiet, "Oh," was all she could say.

Lukos felt his heart jump. His mouth tried to form more words but none of them departed his lips successfully. Her eyes were big and brown and wide, and he couldn't seem to look away from them.

Behind him, the shop door opened, the little bell tinkling again, and Lukos was jarred from his stupor.

"I'm sorry," he repeated. "It was stupid of me, not looking where I stepped."

She blinked twice before smiling at him. "Beg your pardon, sir, don't think of it."

"Move!" grouched the man behind Lukos, exiting the shop. Lukos spun and apologized again, stepping out of the man's way. When he turned back, the lady was already gone. Lukos looked around, certain that he had to find her in the crowd. He felt his spirits drop after being unable to do so.

But even if he had . . . *then what?* Saddened, Lukos looked toward the direction of the Industrial District and began to walk again, with less excitement than before.

He placed a hand over his coat pocket to feel the familiar, comforting weight of his watch. Frowning, he checked his other pocket, then his pant pockets. There was no weight.

Lukos spun in a panic and scoured the ground with his eyes. He was sure it had been with him until now. His eyes traveled over the side street and up into the crowd as he tried to grasp where it could have gone. And then his eyes found her again and, although confused, he had a moment of understanding.

Kit stole a fleeting glance at her mark before cutting a quick path around the corner. His cheeks were a healthy red as he apologized to the man that paid him no mind. A helpless look came over him when he turned again, looking for the girl he had bumped into.

Stop it. Kit shook her head hard, feeling dumb. She was a street thief, and proud of it, not some empty head set to wait on suitors in a pretty parlor. Finished with admonishing herself, she pulled out her only steal that day.

It's not gold, thought Kit, *but I'll take it.*

Retreating deeper into the alley, she looked at her new treasure, a pocket watch. A fine one at that, like no other she had lifted before. It was crafted from silver, and a lot of it. The outer casing bore the carving of a wolf with wings chasing the sun. It was beautiful, fierce. She pressed a button, throwing the hunter-case open. Inside was just as exquisite. Two golden hands ticked over a golden chapter ring, a smaller one giving the month, set on a dial of black obsidian underneath polished crystal. The initials *C.L.* and a date, *May 6, 117*, were carved on the inside of the cover. Underneath it, clearly not professionally etched, but scratched in later, was another date, *Nov. 7, 131*.

The current year was 150, which meant this watch was over three decades old and, except for the scratched in dates, was in near perfect condition. It could not originally have belonged to the man she stole it from. He was far too young. *A family heirloom, perhaps?* It didn't seem old enough for that, either.

Kit shrugged. She would spin it however she had to when the time came to exchange it for some actual gold cards. It was a remarkable find, bringing a rare and genuine smile to her face.

"That's mine," a voice demanded, suddenly behind her. Kit spun, her eyes snapping wide.

They both stood motionless for a moment. Lukos cleared his throat.

"That watch is mine," he repeated.

Kit tried to put on her best smile and took a step back into the alley. Using the same tone and accent as before, she raised her pitch a little for a more gentle, innocent effect. "I found it on the ground. Yours, you say?"

He seemed unsure, but the hint of a smile started to appear on his face. He moved forward, holding out his hand. "Oh, then it is my fault. You'll have to forgive me, I mistook you for a pickpocket. How foolish of me, Miss . . . ?"

He actually bought it? Kit resisted the urge to roll her eyes. *How do the dolts end up with all the money?* She held the watch out to him with her right hand, letting him be the gentleman and walk the rest of the way — which he was, which he did. But as he reached for the watch, her left hand snaked forward and grabbed his wrist, pulling him in. A swift knee landed in his gut with a satisfying thump.

As he sunk to the ground, Kit stowed the watch in her pouch and untied her makeshift dress, throwing the cloak around her shoulders, glad to be able to move her legs more freely again. She swept her hair back and started to climb a drainpipe.

"Stop!"

She ignored him. A hand like a vice grabbed her leg and pulled. Surprised, she turned and kicked, the soul of her shoe meeting his face with an effective smack. He fell back with a grunt. Her shoes were light and thin—he'd get over it with hardly a bruise.

Kit scrambled up the pipe again, but their scuffle proved to be too much for it. It came loose from the fastenings and, with a piercing shriek of metal, crumpled and fell. She landed on her feet, hardly fazed by the fall but irritated nonetheless. Now she had to deal with the rich kid. For an idiot he seemed harmless, but in Limbo you never knew.

He stood slowly and held out a defensive hand. Lukos didn't seem to be bothered by the grime now covering his clothes and hand, or her shoeprint across his face for that matter. She thought it odd for his kind.

"Look, miss. I just want the watch. You're a thief, right? You want money? I can give you money, just give me the watch."

Kit dropped her posh accent in utter shock. "How dare you try to barter for your own possessions? What kind white-livered coward does that?" She tensed, ready to strike the fool again.

"But . . ."

Whatever his argument was, she didn't get to hear it. Kit's pulsed quickened. A drum beat hard in her throat, laced with panic. A shadow blocked the light that filtered into the dirty alley, accompanied by the groaning of metal. One of the large Hollow Men peered at them with its empty black eyes. Steam hissed from its joints, and it began to push forward. The walls shifted, breaking, as metal shoulders made their own room in the narrow space.

You can't be after me.

Lukos felt his entire body tingle, the blood from his extremities seeming to hide in the shell that was his torso. Brick and mortar walls crashed to the ground as the Hollow Man shoved its huge frame further into the alley. Dust and chunks of rough, porous building rained on Lukos as the Hollow reached for him with its long fingers. The world shook from its struggle to advance, filling their only escape from the narrow backstreet.

Fear set in. Stepping back, Lukos spun and saw the pickpocket struggling to kick in a door. It was locked, and far too heavy for her slim figure to knock down. She fumbled with a set a tools, bending to use them on the lock.

Two metal fingers stretched out, and Lukos felt them rip into his back. He growled in pain, but fell toward the girl trapped at the door. "Move!"

She jumped away, looking between Lukos and the Hollow Man with wide, frightened eyes. Lukos punched the door with his left hand, feeling the solid *thunk* of the impact reverberate through him. With a shake of his head, he reared back for another go.

After years of hiding his left hand, he hesitated in front of the girl. The Hollow Man's fingers scratched at the ground near his foot, ridding him of any nervousness. Lukos threw his fist into the door with all of his might, punching a hole through the thick wood. He did it again, this time finding the locking mechanism, ripping the metal from the wood — the door swung open on old hinges.

"How did you do that?" asked the girl, but there was no time. The Hollow was nearly upon them, entire pieces of wall collapsing in its wake. She shoved him inside, a moment before the door and the surrounding wall was bashed in by a giant metal arm. The Hollow's grabbing hand swept just over them, leaving the small supply closet they had entered in wreckage. Further inside the building, shouts of alarm were raised.

Lukos pushed himself up, grabbing the girl by the arms and pulling her to him as stray bricks, broken shelves, and dust continued to storm all around them. "Can you help me get away from it?" he asked. "I can give you gold coins. Please, just hide me."

She frowned, but now was not the time to argue. Grabbing his hand, surprised to feel that it was metal, but warm to the touch, she pulled him out of the supply closet as the Hollow's long fingers ripped an ever-growing hole into the building. It turned out, they had escaped into a cozy saloon. Patrons and owners alike stared and hollered at the two dirty young people that burst into the room amid a billow of dust and debris, marring the sweet, strong aromas.

The place groaned as its alley-side was progressively removed, the pipe organ in the corner smashed under the weight of a toppling bookshelf. A metal claw reached from within the closet, grasping blindly. The woman tending the bar failed to move, and the claw drug gashes over her face and torso, flecks of blood staining the wood in front of her. She collapsed in shock. Her patrons panicked, ducking under the grasping arms of the Hollow Man invading their colorful, happy lives.

"This way!" Kit shouted over the destruction, pulling the

rich young fool toward the front door. The easiest way to escape an Ignavus Hollow was to keep things between them and its large body. Ignavus Hollows were persistent, always pushing forward, but they couldn't chase what they couldn't keep track of. If she could get to the street . . .

A sharpened metal leg crashed through the saloon's front door, and another Hollow Man— this one a spidery Avidum Hollow—birthed itself into the room.

"That can't be right," she told no one in particular. Hollows were solitary enforcers, rarely joining together for any reason. *Why are you two hunting in a pair?*

"We have to go!" her companion yelled, pulling her away from the door.

Kit took another quick look around, pulse beating faster and harder with every click of the Avidum Hollow's insectoid legs striking the tiled floor. She spotted an iron spiral staircase just as the upper level started to lean backward. The giant Hollow was going to bring the place down, and the stairs were bending and tearing with it.

"Everyone get out!" the young man was yelling, warning the patrons. *"Leave!"*

It was a waste of breath, in her opinion, but she wasn't about to waste her own telling him that. At the second floor, she made a beeline for a window-lit room, their gateway to escape.

The Avidum Hollow was already there, its eight legs and four greedy hands propelling its ornate and orb-like body up the stair railing in no time. She ignored it the best she could, nearly dragging her former mark behind her into the room. Kit pushed a small cabinet over, leaning against the door to keep the Hollow out, if even for a moment.

She rushed to the window, throwing it open, looking over her shoulder at Lukos. "Can you climb?"

"Climb? I mean," he stuttered, "a tree, once—"

"Sure, that'll do."

The Avidum exploded through the door, throwing the cabinet aside without challenge. Its greedy claws clicked open and closed in anticipation as lifeless eyes stared back at them.

Kit cursed under her breath. "Time to find out. Do what I do!"

She swung herself from the window, using the ledge

and some shoddy architecture to pull herself up. It was easy enough when the building was falling over, gravity in her favor. She glanced inside the building and saw Lukos lose his footing in the shifting elevation — he slid directly toward the claws of the spider-like Hollow.

Selflessness was not on Kit's list of important qualities. Still, she had lost friends to the Hollows, mostly other thieves. She made a quick decision, dropping onto her belly on the side of a slanting bar, and reached an arm into the window, grabbing her unwanted companion by the scruff of his suit. The Avidum was crawling up the floor, its metal legs digging into the floorboards.

"Thank you for helping me," he said.

Kit gritted her teeth, hauling his weight through the window. "Don't thank me yet."

He grabbed her hand, gave her a sad, thankful look — "Thank you. I mean it," he said, "now run." — and then pried her fingers from his jacket.

Lukos hadn't thought the girl capable of concern, but her eyes widened as he began to fall toward the Hollow again. He was a servant. If they caught him, he'd just be hauled to Lord Doyle, whipped, maybe. A pickpocket, he knew, would be hanged for thievery.

The Avidum Hollow caught him with its four, snapping hands. Lukos felt a pang of regret, wishing he hadn't run into the pickpocket in the first place. If not for her, he would have been able to avoid the Hollows without delay.

He stared at the ornately etched body of the Avidum. This was his first time to see the real deal, and not the black and white pencil sketches on Bell Begor's desk. He suddenly understood why some people feared the simple automatons. With that thought, he resigned himself to being taken back to his surrogate home.

And then the building collapsed.

Chapter Two: Purgatory

Shekelton O'Tool gazed out over Limbo from Oude-monium, as if he could pinpoint the runaway from the city's tallest vantage point. For all of his years of planning and work, he felt a fool to now be set back by something as simple as the boy slipping through Doyle's slack grip.

A lady's cough echoed, just before the clock tower's chimes reverberated through the air, causing his skull to vibrate. The gears and chains above his head continued their chorus of rattling creaks as O'Toole turned and walked back into his office. He closed the door, muting the tower's thoughtful cacophony.

The four nobles seated in his office twitched, shifting. His fellow leaders of the town, allies in the civil war of their youth. Friends and lieutenants. War criminals, really, except that they had won the war.

For all their brave deeds, these four had never felt comfortable in O'Toole's sanctuary, etched with strange sigils and charms as it was. Now with the setback of the servant boy's disappearance, their usual unease had grown to dread. Lord Doyle, in particular, brimmed with nervous frustration. He sat stock straight, feet planted firmly, military habits rising to the surface in this time of crisis.

O'Toole sat down at his desk, fixing his tired, frustrated gaze over Doyle. "This falls on your shoulders."

The thick noble's muttonchops bristled in and out, jaw working. "Be reasonable. The boy has never shown any such indication toward this type of behavior. He's always been quiet and obedient. You would not ask me to watch something as harmless as a rabbit every single second of every day."

"What other task, pray tell, is of such importance to you as to let one charge so easily out of your sight on the very day before he can fulfill our purpose? And this charge, most of all."

"There are nearly twenty young men under my watch,

and th-the Hollow Men—"

O'Toole stood up, reaching across his desk with a long, thin arm. He grabbed Doyle by his large neck and pulled him from his chair, bringing the noble's face dangerously close. "What Hollow Men?" he asked, his voice a menacing rasp. "They have not been manufactured for years."

Doyle seethed, flushed face beginning to sweat.

"Where does this put us?" asked Carlisle, the Land Keeper. "In terms of our plans—our futures—what happens if the boy escapes?"

O'Toole gestured to Shorn. The small man's leg fidgeted like a steamhammer. He sat up on the edge of his seat, feet just landing flat on the ground. "Our best bio-alchemists are close to reaching an alternative solution, should the boy actually escape and Mr. Lucy remain asleep. However, this has never been our main focus, and when I say close, it could very likely take them years."

O'Toole released Doyle and sat down with authority. "Which is time that we simply do not have. Lukos will not escape. There is no place for him to escape to."

"And what of the Fox Den?" Lady Darlington's eyebrow rose.

The archduke exhaled. "If we allow them to touch Lukos, heads will roll, mark my words. Now, I need each of you to go to your district. Lord Doyle has written these up and had the newspapers send out an extra noontime edition for the day. Until that paper is sent out for delivery, though, have your people pass these onto every street corner and newsstand." He pushed forward a small tower of paper—wanted posters.

"This much, just for the kid?" asked Carlisle after seeing the reward money. "Isn't that a bit much?"

"We aren't just talking about Lukos. We are talking about our immortality."

He let that reminder sit with them all.

"I expect you all to draw upon every resource and contact possible to find Lukos. Failure to find him . . ." He paused, looking straight at Doyle. "The consequences will be grave."

Despite his abrasive attitude, Doyle swallowed hard, annunciating the silence of the room.

"Now get out. You four have your work to do, and I

have mine."

Doyle burst from his chair, stiffly marching out the door, in a hurry to redeem himself, the other lords and lady of Limbo not far behind. As soon as the door opened, O'Toole could feel his sanctuary lose its sealed design. A mix of fresh air and oiled machinery rushed in.

As well as other things.

He glared over his desk, quill falling limp in his hand. The slight buzzing of a fly alerted him to the fact that, suddenly, he was not alone.

"What is it, Mr. Zeb? News?"

A voice answered from the darkness behind him, a space previously unoccupied. "Unfortunately."

"Spit it out, then. I do not contract you for your company."

"It was Lukos. We found him in the Arts District, at the edge of Industrial. An Ignavus and several Avidum pursued."

O'Toole sighed. "And this is unfortunate because . . ."

"He escaped."

"He escaped. Again." O'Toole fiddled with the silver

ring around his middle finger. "Are the Ignavus models not persistent enough?"

"This one was too persistent, my lord. Not to fear, though! He was with a girl. Just one more lead to follow."

O'Toole resisted the urge to shudder at the smile in Mr. Zeb's voice. He raised his left hand, letting Mr. Zeb get a good view of his ring. The attendant became silent.

"Industrial, you said. Is Ash ready?"

"She is."

"Good. Get this under control."

Mr. Zeb bowed low, theatric. "Of course, my lord. Your wish is my command."

Kit stood in the shadows, looking back over the rooftops from where she had come. The street corner was layered in a thick dust from the recent collapse.

Shame was not a feeling she was accustomed to dealing with. Whether in stealing or in simply running away to survive, when other thieves had gotten caught, Kit hadn't.

She was the thief who would never be caught.

But why did he tell her to run? No one did that. Not in Limbo.

She slid down to the street level, wrapping her cloak into a faux dress once more. A simple grab here and there and she had some empty-headed lady's hat, and another's purse. The shawl of the third lady was harder to pull off, but Kit was good at her job. She rounded the corner before the women realized they had been robbed blind.

Kit threw the hat on, hiding her eyes and the grime over her face. The purse she let hang daintily from her arm. She would have to be careful — the afternoon crowds were dying down, slinking back to their homes.

It did not take long for her to find the saloon, or what was left. It was a crater now. Hollow Men — of the tall, thin humanoid type, with skull-like faces — dragged bodies from the rubble. The patrons of the saloon. Kit felt anger bubbling up in her stomach, but it was dampened from how often it was she saw people die around Hollows. She shook her head and scanned the bodies, looking for the man she'd stolen the pocket watch from. He wasn't among them, yet.

There was a crowd across the street. She crossed to join them, careful to keep the throng of bodies between the Hollows and herself. She leaned forward to hear two richly dressed young women gossiping in a loud whisper.

"What a scene!" she said, losing her rough street accent and speaking in a slow, lazy manner. "What is all this fuss about?"

One of the chattering ladies, dressed in garish green, addressed Kit in an airy, dismissive way, hardly stopping for breath. "Not the likes we've ever seen! The whole building collapsed. A giant Hollow Man walked up and ripped into the place."

Her friend in purple interjected. "Chasing two street urchins, if what we heard is correct."

"And it isn't! One was a street urchin, the other a handsome young heir. I saw him run from the rubble. Quite a sight. He winked at me."

"No he did not!"

"Did too!"

The green girl and her friend in purple paused to giggle

between each other.

"Anyway, here we are, coming to see what all of the rumbling commotion is, when the whole place nearly crashes down on our head. And all those people, so horrible!"

Kit heard lack of care in the girl's voice and bit her lip to keep from losing her role. "Then . . . he lived?"

"Who?" asked Green.

"The man the Hollows were after."

Purple, "He ran off."

"Did not!" said Green. "I would have run after him."

"Not where he was going. He ran into Industrial." Purple clucked her tongue wisely.

Kit nodded to herself. He had said that was where he wanted to go.

"You were seeing things," said Green.

"Was not!"

Kit stopped listening, her ears beginning to ring as the two women kept arguing. So he was alive. She ducked back, deeper into the crowd, as one of the Hollow Men approached. Everyone shrunk back from it, meaning Kit had to take two extra steps just to feel safe.

It held up a piece of paper. A wanted poster, she realized. Her mark's face was sketched onto it. Above and below his portrait, the poster read:

WANTED. A REWARD OF 50,000 GOLD CARDS WHEN BROUGHT IN ALIVE.

50,000 gold cards! They must have wanted him back very badly.

And alive? In Limbo, that was a rare specification.

Kit hung back. She waited until the crowd grew tired of the spectacle, about the same time that the Hollow Men had finished their investigation of the area. Carefully, as she knew this would make her stand out, she walked up to the building and grabbed one of the several wanted posters that had been glued over the building's face.

Kit didn't know why, but looking at the poster in her hand, she had to find him before anybody else.

Lukos dragged an already damp sleeve across his face. For him, the screams of the people in the saloon hadn't stopped.

He collided with a warm body, mumbling an apology. The other person—a woman with a smudged face and torn coat—kept walking, oblivious. Lukos watched as she shambled along without paying him any mind.

He wore his coat over the shoulders, keeping his left hand deep in its pocket. Without any spare skin to cover the metallic gleam, his hand would remain revealed—and he wasn't sure how people in the outside world would react to a shiny hand. If anything, he doubted it would be a friendly reaction. He shivered in the stagnant, warm air and turned a corner.

A wide thoroughfare opened up before him. Ghostly crowds mingled in the failing light, a flurry of ash dancing over their heads—a symbol of their miserable routine.

The Industrial District.

Finally, he'd made it. He just had not expected it to be this bad.

People drifted past him with sunken eyes and pale faces. They looked strong and wiry, but devoid of life. At least half the people he saw looked unwashed, even under the usual layer of dirt the working class wore. He wondered how many had running water and a regular bath.

Lukos had never been to the Industrial District before. He'd been to Arts and Business, caged inside a carriage, stepping out only to attend to his master. The majority of his life had been secluded within the walls of Doyle's estate inside Residential. This, though, this was different from the other districts. The streets were filthy and caked with soot. Factories were tall and wide, somehow managing to block the view of Limbo's spectacular towers and casting heavy shadows over every block in sight, even while the sun still hung in the sky. Coal fires and bellows gave off an eerie atmosphere, dark with a somber red glow, wheezing silently.

Lukos sighed. This was where he would start his new life.

He needed a job, and a living space — or at least what qualified as such. A guide would be nice, to help him navigate the district. Finding someone friendly here, or even helpful, seemed doubtful.

That was for tomorrow. It would be the beginning of a new year for him. For now he simply hoped to find somewhere he could sleep for the night, maybe find some food. Lukos already missed his kitchen.

An unusual sound tickled his ear—a sad tune with a rapid, steady rhythm. He crossed a street and turned a block to find the musician playing a strange instrument that looked half-piano, half-guitar, and all junk. A dirty, sun-and-sweat-bleached top hat lay on the ground next to the man, whose lank hair swayed to the beat of his own music. Lukos wondered if the man ever actually found any cards, gold or otherwise, in his hat by the end of a song.

It touched his heart. After what he had just lived through, Lukos had emerged into a world of gloom with a new appreciation for life. Trying to be discrete, Lukos took one of his gold coins—one of only three he had left—and bent to drop it into the hat. It fell in with a velvety thud, not meeting any other coins at the bottom.

At the muffled sound, the musician's head snapped

to him, a paranoid look in his eye. After a moment he relaxed and gave Lukos a thankful nod, continuing his melancholy song.

Lukos smiled and nodded back. Behind the man's instrumental setup, on a sooty wall, posters had been tacked up. Performers like the Bearded Lady, penny dreadful plays on the boarder of Industrial and Arts, even propaganda for ways to get more gold cards, such as donating blood, being a test patient in Business, and competing in filthy fighting rings, were all represented by overlapping, half-glued advertisements. Lukos' weary eyes looked over them, then widened at the newest, cleanest spread.

It was his own face there on the poster. A reward was posted below the picture. The sum was too large. He couldn't have been that important to Doyle, or even Bell Begor.

What do you want with me?

He glanced at the musician, whose eyes began to narrow. Inside his jacket, Lukos squeezed his left hand into a ready fist.

He quick-paced across the street, head low. Away from

the musician with his melancholy music, away from his face sketched on the wall. The sun finally disappeared behind the tall town walls, plunging Industrial into premature night. The district was too poor to waste gas for street lamps or safety lighting. Murky green lamps powered by bioalchemic insects sparsely lit the streets instead.

The deeper shadows made him harder to recognize, he knew, but Lukos didn't feel comforted by them. They swelled and flowed like a presence as he passed the burning light of a factory. He felt alone and self-conscious among the burgeoning evening crowd.

"Oy! Oy, yer there!"

Lukos didn't turn around. He flinched when the dirty hand grabbed his arm. The music man spun him around.

"Thanker kindly, good sir. I shan't go hungry t'night, for yer kindness. I just wanted say thank ye."

Lukos smiled. "That is good to hear. I'm glad to know it helped." He tugged away from the man's half-gloves.

"Wait a snip, though," said the musician, squinting. "'Ave we met a'fore? Yer seem familiar to me."

"I would recognize your fine music, I think!" Lukos

embellished, trying to play to the man's graces. "Now if you'll excuse —"

"No, no, t'aint that. I seen yer face before. Wait, I know."

Lukos shoved the man off. "You don't!" he insisted, a little louder than he had meant. Though the street's progress was still moving along just fine, several sets of hungry eyes were trained on him now. The musician shied away with a hurt look in his eyes. From the corner of his eye, Lukos saw a smallish boy with a dirty blue scarf watching them. Seeming to come upon some realization, the boy's eyes grew as wide as his head. He gasped, then ran off. Lukos' eyes flicked back to the musician, who had begun to study him again.

Not good, thought Lukos, *not in the least*. Standing out was not something he could do right now. He pulled his coat tighter, then thought himself a fool for doing so, and began walking away again, a brisker pace this time.

At the next street corner, he chanced a look over his shoulder. The music man was gone.

Lukos let out a sigh, relieved. Too close. The smell of food wafted by him, a bitter thing tinged with the smoke and waste that plagued the air, but food nonetheless. His stomach growled—he hadn't eaten since setting off earlier this morning from Lord Doyle's estate.

It took several minutes to find the source of the odor. The wafting smell led him to a sooty brick wall in the side of some sort of machine shop. Lukos passed by it twice before realizing the scrawny old man sleeping behind the counter was a food vendor. He felt a little guilty to wake the old man up, but the hunger gnawing at his gut was more important right now.

He fished out a gold coin, leaving only one in his pocket, otherwise empty. He sighed in frustration, remembering his thieved pocket watch.

Pushing the image out of his mind, Lukos dropped the gold coin behind the counter, trying for more subtlety than he had with the last vendor. He imagined having money in this part of the town was not a blessing, rather the painted rings on a target. "Can I get something to eat? Please?"

The old man peeked at him from under bushy eyebrows and a soiled hat. His scrawny, lean hand swiped the gold up and he bit it, testing the metal.

"Don' ask please. Sounds rude in these parts. Wot you want, boyo?" Without standing, he opened silver containers inlaid into the counter, revealing gruel, gruel with meat, and meat with gruel.

Lukos' stomach battled his rational mind. "Whatever won't kill me."

The old man laughed a laugh that told of his resignation to life's harsh realities, spooning some of the gruel—without the meat—into a ruddy plastic bowl. "You's in the wrong place, boyo."

"Ah, where is the spoon?" asked Lukos as he took the bowl.

A scruffy, raised eyebrow was his answer.

Was this really what I wanted? thought Lukos as he crossed the street, letting himself slide against the wall to a seated position on the black-caked sidewalk. He looked at the bowl of slop before him, then took in the view of the misery around him. *Maybe I acted too rashly, leaving.*

He missed the comfort of his old home, even if he was just a servant who was worked around the clock putting up with the likes of Lord Doyle.

Why would they send Hollow Men after me, and reward posters? Lukos' mind began to wander to his time spent in service at Doyle's estate. *Why watch me in the shadows of the kitchen, whisper conversations about me until I walked into the room? Didn't they know I could hear them, see them?* He had thought little of it. It was a servant's life to be looked down upon, gossip behind his back spreading here and there, wasn't it?

But then the memories of the red room flooded his mind, making him gag.

Lukos sighed again, shoved the disturbing memories from his mind, and raised the bowl to his lips. He didn't get a chance to taste the mush before it was knocked from his hands —— an unfortunate waste of his coin, and yet, perhaps, quite a fortunate turn of events. Lukos found himself held against a wall.

"Knew it was yer!" the music man spat at him, an almost frenzied look in his eye. His right hand held Lukos to the wall, his left hand clutching a wanted poster. *His* wanted poster.

"Don't know whot yer did, mister, but then again, 'ardly matters . . . I'm cashin' yer in for that reward."

Lukos panicked. Inside his coat sleeve, his metal hand flexed. But he couldn't harm this man in the street. That would be wrong. And yet, aside from his left hand, he knew he didn't have the strength or skill to get away from the musician.

"All my sufferin's are endin'," sang the music man, and Lukos couldn't help but pity him. That is, until he began dragging Lukos forward. "Soon as that fifty's mine!"

Something metal and of moderate size flashed behind the music man, accompanied by a pleasant gong-like sound. His grip on Lukos' jacket collar slackened, and the music man fell to the ground with a grunt. Before Lukos could comprehend what had happened, the thief — the one who'd pinched his pocket watch — was standing there. She held pans in both hands, watching the downed, and deeply breathing, musician carefully. Beside her, the wide-eyed boy with the blue scarf Lukos had seen earlier clutched another one of the wanted posters.

"See, Kit," he said, "there he is!"

For a moment, she smiled at the young boy, and Lukos stifled a breath. He absently wondered how such a dazzling smile could survive in this district. She patted the boy on the head.

"Good job, Biggy. Run along now. This one's danger-ous."

The boy called Biggy smiled, putting his hands on his hips. "Then I'll stay an' protect you!"

"I can handle him. Now, you," she said, glaring at Lukos, "come on and hurry up."

All bright smiles and gentle words having vanished, the thief turned and walked to the vendor, returning the metal pans. "Thanks for this, Mr. Mood. I promise, I didn't put any of those dents in."

"Anytime, Kit. Keep yourself safe this evenin', girly. There's trouble about tonight."

"Don't worry about me."

"All right, all right! Just sayin', is all."

Kit began to walk away and noticed Lukos across the street. Realizing he hadn't moved an inch, she let out a soft growl and held up a finger, hooking it into a silent command: *Here, now!* Lukos nearly tripped over the music man to get to her.

"Thanks," he said in a whispered rasp.

She shook her head. "You stand out like some battered thumb, you know that?"

"I was trying to blend in," he spluttered. "They . . . they have my face . . ."

"Yeah. Saw that. And your name. What kind of a name is Lukos?"

"What kind of a name is Kit?"

She glared at him, her scrutiny lasting too long. "Maybe you're not as dumb as you look. But you aren't smart, either. You stand out. People know you don't belong here, they're going to figure out pretty quick it's you on the posters. You got any more valuables in that coat of yours?"

He eyed her warily. "Why?"

She eyed him back. "Relax. I'll not take anything else from you. I'm trying to help. So if you got anything you might, say, wanna keep on your person, I would suggest taking it out now and putting it in a different pocket."

Lukos didn't know what she was up to — if any-thing — but he was at a loss in his situation. He palmed his last gold coin and stuck his hands in his pants pockets.

"Okay," he said.

"Right on time. How did you get away from those Hollows, by the way?"

He felt his throat swell up, remembering the bodies sticking out here and there in the rubble of the gift shop. "They were caught under the rubble. I ran before they could get out."

"Good. Survival is of the utmost."

"But all of the others . . ."

"Others?"

"The other people. Did you hear their screams?"

"Why do you care?" she asked, suspicious.

The blackened cobbles under his feet blurred as his mind kept flashing back to that scene. A grip on his arm stopped him and he looked up, surprised to see Kit looking at him.

"Hey." There was a tenderness under her irritable tone. "Stop it."

Lukos looked at her with blatant confusion, stomach churning. "Stop what?"

"Thinking about them. They're dead. There isn't anything you could have done. That's what happens when Hollow Men are around."

He felt his ears burn. "I can't just forget something like that."

"Don't forget. But move on. Keep going."

Lukos' eyes watered. He searched her face for answers she didn't have. Their eyes locked. She blinked and let go of his arm, taking a step back. Kit shook her head, "It's, uh . . . anyway, it's right up here."

Lukos was about to ask what when she walked around the corner. He followed and found himself being introduced.

"Okay, Lukos — it is Lukos, right? — this is George. George, Lukos needs something to eat. Caught him trying to get at one of Mood's bowls. Saved him just in time."

They were at the mouth of an alleyway, the alternating sounds of wheezing bellows were loud from the buildings overhead. Lukos was greeted by a boy hardly twelve years old, who looked him over studiously from atop a pile of bundled newspapers, sitting in front of a larger-than-life, communal rubbish bin. "How d'ya do?" the boy asked in an important voice. Then the boy looked at Kit. "Payment?"

Kit grabbed Lukos by the shoulders — "Hey, wait! What are you doing?" — and spun him around. The next thing he knew, Lukos was out of a coat. His left hand glinted dully in the low light from the factories, and he was sure someone on the street would notice its rarity. However, as he looked around, self-conscious, no one seemed to pay him any mind. Even the thief and the self-important boy seemed more enthralled with Lukos' well-made coat than his hand.

". . . a little banged up, but it can be mended. It's good and warm. Wha'do you say, Georgie?"

"Don't call me Georgie, Kit! Bad for business. It's just George now."

The girl rolled her eyes, and the boy nodded to himself seriously.

"I'll take it," he said, finally. "I'd say for a silver piece's worth."

Lukos raised his hand to say that the suit was easily worth several gold pieces, but Kit kept going.

"He'll also be needing a replacement. And shoes. And I need some food."

George tilted his head down, fixing her with a pointed stare. "There wasn't no such deal."

Kit sighed but produced a lady's purse and scarf. "There was a hat, too, but I lost it."

"I dunno. There isn't much here, Kit." The boy dug through the purse, pulling out a handkerchief, some makeup, a picture of a loved one.

"Come on, Georgie. Take out the gold pieces if you want. My business wasn't so good today. I wasted it on . . . well, never mind it, it just wasn't good. And we—I—had to dodge some Hollows. Besides, you owe me a favor. For past times and like."

"Past times my arse." The boy sighed but nodded. "Just this once. But I'll hold you to a favor of your own this time."

"Thanks kindly, lil' sir! You know I'm good for it."

Giving her another unimpressed stare, George hopped down from his pile of papers and walked around the rubbish bin. He came back out moments later with a loaf of bread, boots, and a dirty coat.

"I'm supposed to wear that?" Lukos asked, causing the thief and her friend to stop, turn, and give him a severe look over.

"Have a problem with that?" she asked.

Lukos felt his cheeks warm. "Of course not. I'm sorry, that came out wrong. I just . . . it looks . . . warm. Cozy."

"Bricks, you're horrible at lying. Come on, let's get you outfitted."

He hesitated, and she gave him an impatient look. Finally he relented, thrusting his left hand into the jacket so that he didn't keep it exposed. She gave him a knowing look. "I'll need to know about that later," she whispered, brushing close to his ear while crossing behind to put his right arm into the musty coat. "Later, when no one else will try and cut that hand off of you."

Lukos shivered, but said nothing. Next were the boots.

"He's kind of a heavy stepper as it is," Kit said, thinking aloud. "Got anything lighter, George?"

The boy answered with another dull glare.

Lukos pulled off his remaining shoe—the one he had

not lost scaling up the side of the gift shop — and slipped on the heavy leather, tying the ratty laces firm. *At least they don't smell as bad as they look.*

When he'd finished, they thanked George, took the bread, and moved on, with Lukos following the pickpocket once more. She ripped the bread in two and handed him the smaller piece, stuffing her mouth as she walked. He wondered how much the girl's thinness had to do with being a lithe thief, and how much it had to do with having nothing to eat.

Lukos looked at the half-torn loaf in his hand. He thought of the feasts he had helped to prepare at Lord Doyle's estate. It seemed so little, and he nearly swallowed it whole.

He slowed his chewing so as to enjoy what he could of stale bread, then dared a glance at the pretty pickpocket next to him. "So, Kit . . ."

He waited. No response. He tried again.

"Thanks. For the help, I mean."

Industrial's ambient wheezing and clanking metal accentuated the gaps in his conversation.

"I noticed your speech is impeccable. Very proper. Better than I would think for a street thief."

"If you're trying to pay me a compliment, it isn't working."

He blushed. "Just curious, was all. Wondered where you picked it up."

"Does it matter?" Not for the first time that day, she turned abruptly, pushing Lukos into the shadowy embrace of a less-than-alluring alleyway.

"What I want to know," she said, "is what you are and who you are, and why the blazes you're setting the Hollow Men off their normal selves in the Arts District!"

He kept his mouth shut, and allowed his mind to work to figure out which question to answer first.

A bundled figure, all scruff and beard and soiled attire passed by the alley, dragging along slowly, without cause or urgency of direction. They both watched as his wrinkled face turned toward them, then moved on in that same indifferent pace.

Kit looked back at Lukos, rolling her eyes. "So I guess you rich'ens aren't so smart after all. Let's start with what you are. Are you part automaton, or some new sort of Hollow Man they've created? I'll bet that's it, isn't it?" she asked, put off by the idea.

"What? No. I'm human, of course," he replied in an offended tone. "And my lack of words has nothing to do with my intelligence, but rather your—"

"Save it for someone who cares. If you're human, why does your hand look like something I might want to steal?"

Lukos sighed. He checked the alleyway's entrance again to make sure no one was watching, then lifted his arm and pulled the frayed sleeve back. Some of the synthetic skin still hung in places around the palm and back of his hand. He peeled the remainder of it off.

He was surprised at how she didn't seem bothered by it, at all. If anything, she was puzzled. He bent his gleaming fingers back and forth—they were still sore from dismantling the doors earlier that day.

"It's different, I know," he said as her hand slowly reached forward. Her finger hovered over the ridgelines on the inside of his palm—they were the same as the lines on anyone's palm, more like skin than metal. Lukos shivered.

She glared at him, suspicious again. Her hand dropped. "Different? Yes. What is it, though?"

"It's metal. That's the only way I know how to describe it."

"But it's impossible. There are no separated joints or pieces. It looks like . . . metal *skin*."

Lukos nodded. "That's exactly what it is. I still feel with my hand. And that includes pain. It's just stronger than your average limb. More durable."

"But how?"

He tucked his hand back in the sleeve and smiled sadly, wishing he knew himself. Clearly this was too much for her. "That's something I aim to find out."

"Is that why the Hollows are after you?"

"I don't know that either." A frown fell on his face, and anxiety began to brew in his stomach. Memories of the last few months in Lord Doyle's estate flooded him — the strange looks they had begun to level at him, whispers in hallways. Menacing whispers: *Is it ready yet? The boy will be of age soon.* "I don't think so."

"So wait." Kit waved her hands around. "Back up! Who are you, really? Heaven knows why a rich brat like you would want to come to a hell like Industrial."

Lukos frowned. "I'm not rich. Just a servant who works the kitchen."

She laughed, disbelieving. "Right. Just the cook." She stopped when he nodded sincerely. "Who dresses their cook like you? You looked more the master. And trust me, I've robbed 'em all," she said with a wicked grin.

"I served tea. I didn't buy the suit."

"Who was your master?"

"Lord Doyle."

Kit gasped. "No!"

"Well, yes."

"That old bastard? The noble who makes the Hollow Men?"

"Well . . ." Lukos knew the truth, of course. It had been Miss Begor that was the mastermind behind the Hollow Men designs and models. Doyle was just the businessman who owned the factories. The political figure for people to identify with. "Somewhat, yes."

Kit walked further into the alley, finding an empty crate and sitting on it, sweeping her cloak to the side. "Still doesn't make sense, though. Why did you run away?"

He pictured the dying animal in that horrid room, thinking, *So that didn't become me.* He told her the simpler truth: "Freedom."

She laughed a shallow, breathy laugh, eyeing him. "*Freedom?* Well, welcome rich cook servant. Welcome to so-called freedom. Purgatory, more like."

What came next should have been easy for Kit. It was for her own survival, after all, and for the poor souls of Industrial. Lukos was bad news to them all, thanks to the price on his head. Hollow Men had killed carelessly in the Arts District to catch him. She could only imagine what they would do in Industrial.

And yet, her decision didn't come easy. While she didn't fully trust him, she couldn't help but feel that he believed every word he said. Something about his face said he wouldn't be able to lie to save the world. As he stood there with eyes still reddened by tears — tears over the death of people he didn't even know — Kit couldn't help but see one of the cleanest, brightest souls she'd ever met in all of Limbo. Not even children like George seemed so innocent. Lukos scared her, and fascinated her.

She could hardly make up her mind. The mantra of the strong: *Only the strong need to survive*, allowed Kit to turn her back on him. "You don't belong in Industrial. You should leave."

"What?"

"We have enough problems without the likes of you causing us more."

"I don't understand."

"Hollow Men are after you. You're upset about them bringing a roof down on some shop? It'll happen again, and it will be worse for Industrial. So . . . out you go."

"Just like that?"

"Yes. No. I almost forgot." She took something out of her purse, holding it out to him. It was his pocket watch. "This is yours. I don't know why it's so important to you and I don't really care anymore. Just leave Industrial."

Lukos grabbed the timepiece eagerly, although she didn't let go. They locked glances, and she found his gaze to be too innocent, too honest. She looked away and let the Albert chain drop. Lukos held it close, fingers running over the warm, engraved silver, looking on as Kit took one step, then another.

"Wait!"

Kit bit her lip, pausing. *Brickit, girl.* So much for her big decision.

"Please," he begged. "I just need some help. Help me find a place to stay and a place to work and I'll be out of your hair. I'll stay clear. If I were to go to one of the other districts, they would find me."

She sighed. "Oh, without a doubt. Problem is, the Hollows will find you here too. But they won't hold back and play good like they do in your nicer districts. Here, they'll punish anyone else around you."

"What are you on about?" he scoffed. "Hollows don't play, and they don't lash out at those who haven't done anything against the law. They aren't nice, or mean, or anything in between. They don't have personalities at all—"

"You're wrong."

"Don't be silly. Listen to me, I know. Remember, I lived with their designer. I've seen the prototypes built. Each Hollow has an artificial homunculus placed inside to power and pilot it—"

"Have you ever seen them built?" She paused. "I didn't think so."

They were interrupted as Biggy ran up, huffing. Kit tried to forget about Lukos for a second, leaning down as her street fellow doubled over, hands on his knees. "What's wrong, Biggy?"

He took a gasping breath before looking up, his eyes their usual oversized ovals. "I've been looking for you everywhere!"

"Well, here I stand."

"Kit, you've got to hide."

"Why, Biggy?"

Immediately she tensed. Tensed for the news she had been expecting, but wasn't ready for.

"The Hollows are on the streets." Biggy held up a

wanted poster, but this time Lukos' face wasn't the only one printed there. "And now they're looking for you, too, Kit."

There she was, her face marking the dull paper. Her worst fear as a thief, finally come to fruition. Kit forced down the rising panic. She'd always been so careful.

That wasn't completely true. She took risks, venturing outside of Industrial for her "business," but she had never been spotted, and certainly never a posted criminal. Her face was never seen. She wondered if it was when the building came down, or when she saved him from the maddened musician. Gossip spread fast in Limbo. Now she was stuck in the same burning house with Lukos, and the flames just got hotter. If she had just left him alone, walked away.

"All right," she said to no one particular. "All right. There has to be a way out of this one."

"Kit, you didn't hear me. They're on the streets. Now! You gotta go hide."

She nodded briskly, shooing the boy away. "Don't be anywhere around the Hollows, Biggy, got it? I'll be fine.

Go, already!"

Biggy nodded, nearly tripping over himself as he began to run backward. She watched to make sure he got to the other side of the street quickly, vanishing into the shadows. *Good boy*, she thought.

Then she whipped around, jabbing a finger in Lukos' chest. "You're in deep," was all she mustered, voice faltering when she saw his frightened eyes.

Kit tried her hardest to ignore Lukos' infuriating naivety as she grabbed him by the shoulder of his coat and began to drag.

"Shouldn't we go deeper into that alley?" he asked as they walked past one of the green bug-lit lamps.

"No. That way is a dead end. There's someone who can help us for tonight. The only person I know in Limbo that the Hollows don't go poking around too much. If we can only get there in time."

Up ahead, a tall, slim figure walked out into the street and Kit cursed under her breath. It might have looked human with its black trench coat and bowler hat, but Kit recognized the stiff movements. She pulled Lukos and herself into a darkened doorway just as she saw two eyes like fire begin to glow under the brim of its hat.

"What was that?" Lukos asked in a whisper.

"You mean you don't know? So much for living with Doyle. That was a Hollow Man."

"There isn't a Hollow with glowing red eyes. All of their eyes are, well, hollow."

"And yet, there he was."

She pulled him along, feeling her way through the dark. This was a housing building she knew, and not one of Industrial's safest. The gas-powered light—one of the few in the district—was shut off often, making it a place of commerce for those in the synthetic substance trade. A paranoid, nervous group. Not a crowd that Kit liked to associate with.

Better to meet the engineer junkies than the Hollow Man behind them, she thought. A faint shuffle came from somewhere before them in the darkness. Kit swallowed her fear and inched forward, her hand still on Lukos' shoulder. She stumbled into a rubbish bin, knocking it over. The clang was deafening.

"What was that?" Lukos asked in a loud whisper.

"Relax," she told him, trying to calm her own drumming heart. "It was me."

"Relax. Yes. I'll work on that."

An angry, but weak-sounding voice called out. "Who's there?"

"Sh!" said Kit, taking a risk. "There's a Hollow outside."

It worked. Kit thought she could make out the overturned can and its contents, a drab shape just beyond. As quietly as possible, she moved behind it, tugging Lukos along with her. The shape turned out to be stairs.

They peered over the top of the steps. Two red lights appeared in the doorway leading out, and they both ducked. Something breathed heavily at the door. Then it growled, perhaps in frustration, metallic footsteps grating over the cobbled street as it walked away. It was the Hollow Man, Kit knew. She wondered if Lukos still believed they were just homunculi inside after hearing that.

"What was out there?"

Kit rolled her eyes. She refused to respond to any more of his questions at the moment. "Just follow me. It's you they want, so if they catch you, I'm running on."

"Thanks for that."

They crept back to the door, this time avoiding the overturned can and its disarrayed contents. Kit leaned out and snuck a peek around. No one in sight.

Don't get caught, she reminded herself. *Ever.*

She took off running.

Lukos realized Kit was running. He took a jolting leap after her, missing the few steps leading from the building, landing on the cobbled street in a race of his own. She was much faster, and the thick boots weren't helping. He prayed with all his might that she would at least stay within his line of sight.

Red eyes glowed ahead. Kit took a turn so fast that Lukos barely caught it. He skidded to a halt, eyes lingering too long upon the rail-thin creature. This one wore a hood. It growled at him, and he quickly turned and fled, finding Kit once again.

That's no Hollow, thought Lukos. This was a monster straight out of one of his favorite books in Lord Doyle's library. Only, whatever it was, he would much rather be reading about it than being chased by it.

It seemed to Lukos that they ran the distance through Industrial, ducking under hanging hooks and dilapidated support beams, holes in brick walls. The factories continued to belch steam and smoke amidst an endless clanging of metal, but the streets were dead. Not a soul in sight. They knew, he thought. The people of this district knew when they shouldn't be out on the street.

They came to a strange building that stood out against the others in Industrial. It wasn't very big, but it had a few stories and looked cleaner than the other buildings, and real gas fires lit its perimeter. A large sign with a woman's silhouette hung on its face. It read: *The Rusted Rose.*

And Kit was running right to it.

A pair of red eyes at his right. Lukos glanced behind him and saw that the other creature was still following him, while another far off to the left came around the corner. So there were more than one, and they were closing in.

Kit rammed into the doorframe. Lukos skidded to a halt behind her as she banged both fists on the copper.

A slit in the door was opened. "Who is it?"

"It's Kit, let me in!" she cried, desperate. From inside, someone saw the Hollows, swore, and shouted, "Go get Ash!"

Lukos turned once in a full circle, watching as the creatures began to speed up, their awkward height making them look as if they were loping along or taking the disjointed strides of some sort of giant bird. He flexed his left hand—still sore—and took one look at the door, ready to tear it open.

He yelped as something grabbed his shoulder—cold, hard, and violent. Being whipped around, Lukos found himself face to face with his enemy. So close—horribly close—Lukos finally saw what was under the bowler cap. But it made no sense to him.

Its head was shaped into a metal skull, the distinctive face of the common enforcers of the city—the Callidus model, the very last type of Hollow Man to be produced years ago.

Kit had been telling the truth, it was a Hollow after all. And yet, in those black empty sockets, two crimson eyes stared out at him, burning like eclipsed suns. A deep growl came from within the creature, sounding more like a feral animal than a homunculus grown in a jar.

It isn't possible, thought Lukos, his conversation earlier with the thief coming back to him. Possible or not, Lukos found himself afraid. Not just afraid of being taken back to Doyle, but of this machine—and whatever was inside it.

And then it let go of him. Lukos stumbled back, terrified and now surprised as the Callidus took a step away from him. Two hands, human this time, pulled him from the monster, away from the outside world and in through the door, slammed promptly behind him.

Lukos and Kit both lay on the floor, breathing hard. The room was spacious, some sort of establishment with chairs and tables, and a bar, and a stage. The music was loud, a woman singing passionately with musicians who were playing their stringed instruments too hard. Everything was lit or shaded in reds and pinks and whites.

"We should keep moving," he said, trying to stand. He found himself yelling to be heard over the music and a crowd's ruckus. "That won't keep them for long."

"Quite the contrary, love." The woman at the doorway shook her head. "You're safe in here." She was the most beautiful woman Lukos had ever seen, the soft curve of her lush lips a stark contrast to her bright, piercing blue eyes. Light brown locks fell over her strong shoulders, cascading across the softness of her breasts, barely held in by her intricate turquoise dress. Her tall form continued down with gentle curves, lace and folds clinging to midriff, thighs, and —

Lukos looked away, his ears burning. Her beauty was commanding, causing Lukos to feel sensations that he had never paid attention to. He tried to focus on this new place. *Where am I?*

It was crowded. The high-ceiling did nothing to help relieve the crush of body heat and loud conversations. Lukos could see a bar on one side of the room where a scantily-dressed woman served drinks. On the far opposite wall, several women danced to the seductive rhythm of a ragtime piano in various degrees of clothing, or lack thereof. One slipped out of her top, tossing it to the howling crowd as she waggled her shoulders — and now-bared bosoms. Lukos looked away, growing warmer by the second.

He looked to Kit, his anchor of safety. "Why are we here?"

She stood, still panting. "The Hollows don't mess with this place. Haven't the brickiest why, but they don't. Perhaps they're just afraid of her."

"Of who?" asked Lukos.

Kit walked up to the woman and gave her a hug. "Of the scariest woman in Industrial, that's who. Lukos, meet Ash."

Chapter Three: Rust and Fire

"L ukos," Ash rolled off her tongue.

Kit watched Ash give Lukos a studious onceover. "How lovely to meet you."

"Very nice to meet you as well." Lukos yelled over the racket behind him. He continued to stare at the door, which, for the moment, remained sealed behind her. "They won't come in?"

"They? Oh, the Hollows?" The woman laughed daintily, setting Kit at ease. "Don't worry about them. They know better than to test their mettle with me."

"We need your help," urged Kit.

"Yes you do! Of that I'm sure. You and this fine young boy are all that Limbo has been talking about tonight. It isn't like you, my sweet. I expected you to sneak in the back, normal like."

"No time to come around. The Hollows were sticking pretty close."

"Oh, I know, dear. Think of this, the stubborn Kit finally needs my help. Never thought the day would come. Now, if only you would take me up on my job offer—"

Kit frowned. "That answer is still no. Will you hide us?"

Ash smiled, her white teeth shining through deep red lipstick. "'Course, love. Let's talk back stage where we can hear ourselves think, yes?"

Ash sashayed past them, her presence causing the crowd to divide. Men and women both watched her with a palpable hunger, yet respectfully, almost reverently, made room for her passage. Kit pulled Lukos along behind, keeping up with the overpowering woman in blue.

He passed, coughing through a cloud of cigar smoke mixed with the fragrance of sweet pipe tobacco, only to be assaulted by the odor of a man's sour sweat. Perfume was next, heady and deliberate. A woman crossed in front of him in a bright corset and a faux-jewel encrusted bird mask making sure he was to understand her fragrance, and her skill set. She smiled at him, too sweetly. Scents, emotions, and a dazzle of curiosity ripped through Lukos' mind and body, inviting him to a new world and its spirituous desires and liturgy.

"What kind of theater is this?" he asked Kit, eyes watering and scratching a sudden itch behind his ear.

The street thief looked at him with something between concern and amusement. "Theater? Throw a brick," she exclaimed. "You uninitiated soul! Lukos, this is a brothel."

Eyes darting around the room, Lukos tried to avoid watching the women on stage, nearly every one of them now bared for all of Limbo's willing and desirous to see. But the rest of the room was no safer. Couples and small groups could be picked out amongst the warm throng of people and in the corners, at the bar, or lounging on couches, engaged in passionate exchanges of lips, hands, and teeth, their clothing becoming disheveled or removed altogether, faces flushed, consciousness altering into blissful, frenzied exultations by the second.

Eventually he glued his eyes to the back of Kit's head as best he could. Intoxicating sensations pounded inside his head, and elsewhere. The stimuli were new, and much too overwhelming to ignore by his own devices.

"Oh," he said, continuing to rub behind his ear.

Ahead of them, Ash chuckled. "Haven't you ever seen a brothel, Lukos?"

"No."

"Ah." Her eyes fluttered seductively. "We can give you the grand tour—"

"I think rest would do fine," Kit interjected. Lukos caught her worried look and smiled appreciatively.

Ash looked over her shoulder with a sly smirk. "A little peeking through the window never hurt anyone. Just a look?"

"No," Lukos said again, firm this time.

"A strange one you found there, Kit," said Ash with a pout. "Just your rooms, then."

They finally passed through the greasy crowd and Lukos took a deep, cleansing breath, happy to walk through the door leading backstage. "You'll have to excuse the mess," Ash warned them. "Running an establishment like mine, you don't have much time to keep clean."

Lukos was about to assure her it didn't matter when they passed through the backstage dressing room. He immediately looked down again, following Ash and Kit's feet closely amongst a chorus of squeals and giggles from the brothel girls.

"Warn us next time, Miss Ash!" one called.

"Oh, he's a cute one."

"Are we doing a backstage show tonight?"

Ash raised her hands, motioning for them to be quiet. "Settle down, ladies, settle down. Just another urchin with no place to stay."

Lukos recognized one of them—Lily, a frequent visitor of Doyle's mansion. They locked eyes, but the girl didn't say anything, instead nodding her head silently and looking back at her vanity mirror.

Ash's girls continued to giggle and tease until they entered a tiny hallway, which Lukos found had more breathing space than the larger rooms before it. It was quiet here, enough to hear laughter and other, more intimate sounds from the floor above them.

"Here we are," said Ash, coming to a couple of doors. "The spare rooms aren't much, but they'll do for a place to hide and sleep. This place used to be a hotel before the civil war. The upper rooms I renovated for clients, but these I use for storage and the occasional soul that needs hiding. They're used for storage mostly, but they'll at least have beds."

She threw the doors open to the rooms. There was a small mattress in each, dusty furniture, trunks, and other miscellaneous items piled in the corners.

"Trust me, I'm used to worse," said Kit. "It'll be great. Thanks, Ash."

"Yes. Thank you," said Lukos rigidly. "If you don't mind, I will take my leave."

The brothel owner nodded. "Go and rest, Lukos. I fear a great ordeal lies directly ahead of you."

He felt a tinge of fear, seeing the honesty in her pale face. "Goodnight to you both. Thank you, again. For everything." He made his way into the room and closed the door behind him, standing there in the dark. Lukos' eyes slowly adjusted and he moved to the bed.

Sitting on the edge of the bed, he tried not to listen to the lewd sounds above him. Blocking out one set of unsettling sounds only led to another though. He began to hear the screams of innocent people dying again, felt the sensation of the floor fall beneath him as he relived that moment in the saloon; feeling the horror when he opened his eyes after blacking out from the fall, seeing the crushed forms all around him.

The Hollows. They had acted consciously, with purpose and thought.

Whatever drove the Hollow Men were not homunculi. Kit was right—he was putting everyone else in danger here. *What about Lord Doyle and Bell Begor? How much did they, and the other nobles, know about the Hollow Men? How much did they hide from the people of Limbo?*

Don't be an idiot, he thought to himself. *Of course the nobles know.* The red room, the animal's throat being cut . . . now the Hollows . . . *Who are the nobles, anyway?* Lukos felt like there was a much larger game being played than anyone realized.

He shook his head, trying to jar the troubling thoughts and images from his mind. Lying back, he tried complaining to himself about how the bed reeked and was lumpy and old. The noises from above his ceiling were less horrid now, if yet still embarrassing. He blushed, but took it all in, content not to think of the evils that had shaken his world in the last day.

It felt strange, not bathing before bed, no brushing his teeth or any of his other evening rituals to keep. No midnight snacks for Lord Doyle, no staring at the ceiling processing the mundane events of his day, nor dreaming of the day he would venture beyond the walls of Doyle's estate.

That day had finally come, and it certainly didn't align with his dreams.

What did I do wrong? Lukos stopped himself there. Self pity would get him nowhere, and any questions that might lead him to the answers he wanted had already chased each other around his head throughout the course of this hellish day. Worrying about things he could not control now would only serve to hinder his survival.

Instead, he mentally checked off a long list of chores and duties and repetitions he wouldn't have to worry about tonight. The mental list somehow brought him a sense of comfort, familiarity. Lukos was asleep before he'd thought through half of it.

"What are you doing, Kit? Since when do you hang around people with rewards on their head?"

"Couldn't say myself, really," Kit looked at the floor, a little hurt by her friend's disappointed tone. This was a woman who accepted everyone for who they were. After a moment, Ash smiled sadly and patted her on the arm.

"Come on. Let's have a spot and you can tell me how all of this happened."

Ash led the young pickpocket through her establishment.

"Hey Kit," called Jasmine. One of Ash's pride and joys — olive-skinned, voluptuous, and always willing to go the distance for service callers. A brothel girl—she was about Kit's age. "Joining the house, yet? You know redheads get all the love."

Kit frowned. "You know I won't, Jas. Why don't you come out and help me make a living some time?"

"Can't do that," Jasmine said with a halfhearted laugh. "They'll string you up if they ever catch you."

"I'd rather steal than let some Dark Cully handle me." She shrugged as Ash raised an eyebrow at her. "No offense."

Jasmine's shoulders followed the waggling of her eyebrows. "It isn't so bad. You might even find you like it." She let out a sultry sigh before blowing a kiss toward Kit.

Kit waved her off and chuckled, then greeted a handful of other girls as they walked through the thin hallways, never delving into the conversations they attempted to start. She was glad when they reached Ash's room.

For the mistress of the house, Ash's private dwelling space was humble. It was small and cramped, full of strange books and stranger paintings that told stories of a world vibrant and alive with plants and animals—before the time of the Great Destruction. It smelled of roses, forgoing the other odors that Kit always picked up on when she was visiting the Rusted Rose.

Ash patted her luxurious bed and smiled at Kit, then crossed to the cupboard. "What flavor tonight, Miss Kit?"

"You know I don't care," said Kit, watching Ash's lithe movements. Everyone fell in love with Ash — she was otherworldly. While Kit held no interest in women, the overwhelming woman was still enjoyable to behold as she danced around, fiddling with different flavors of tea.

"Come now. I'm trying to culture you, dear."

Kit snorted, taking a seat on the bed's corner. "What use is that to me? I have enough culture to blend in when I need to. Just give me a drink."

"Manners, now, manners."

"A drink. *Please.*"

Ash sighed, and they both relented. She put a pot on the boiler and gave Kit a worried look. "So tell me what happened."

Kit sighed and then launched into it. "I thought he was an idiot with money. It was supposed to be an easy job."

She told her story and Ash listened, sympathetic, without interrupting. That was Ash for you.

Kit didn't care for her business—becoming a prostitute was another way of giving in to O'Toole and Doyle and the other nobles. Giving in to Limbo. Kit preferred to take, rather than give. Even so, she respected the girls of the Rusty Rose. They were always there for the street urchins and people not fortunate enough to find work in the factories. If one wasn't up to the task of being a girl of the house, there were other careers in Ash's employ—couriers, information brokers, lookouts, all threads in a giant web of knowledge and intrigue, and a significant leverage of power. She was always there when the people of Industrial needed her.

Kit laid her hands on her lap, having divulged her last detail. "And here we are."

The pot screamed at them, hissing steam escaping as the water boiled. Ash shook her head, turning around to pour two cups. "What do you mean, we? Kit, you can't really be putting yourself along with this boy, can you?"

"I certainly wasn't, but it's been done. I didn't choose it."

"There is always a choice."

Kit sighed, knowing all too well about choices. She had left out the part about trying to find and help Lukos in the first place.

"Listen here," Ash continued, looking over her shoulder. "I know what the nobles want. They don't care about you, Kit. They just want Lukos. You can still make a run for it. When they find him—and they will find him—you'll not have to look over your shoulder."

Kit felt some of the tension release from her shoulders at the thought of a way out. And yet, what was that feeling at the bottom of her stomach? *Don't ask.*

She fidgeted with a hole in her coat.

"Why?"

"Pardon?"

"Why? That reward is insane for someone like him. The nobles, they must be desperate. What do you know, Ash?"

Ash shook her head, scooping an extra spoon of honey into her tea. She handed one of the cups to Kit. "You don't want to know, Kit. Not this time. This is nasty business. Grotesque and unrelenting."

Kit sipped at the steaming cup. The taste was nice, probably. Refined, she was sure. But she didn't really care for it. "I don't know. It doesn't seem right, just letting him be taken off like that. He said he's a cook. A servant. I can't imagine they'd send that many Hollows out for just some servant boy to fix dinner. Whatever they have in store for him, it isn't—"

"Don't!"

Kit looked at her friend, eyes wide.

"I'm warning you right now, girl. Don't get involved. Don't even think about it. In fact, don't stay here tonight. Leave, before they come for him. My door won't stay locked to them forever."

"You mean, you're going to turn him in? For what, the money?"

Ash's eyes burned underneath their heavy lashes. "It's not like that. You know me, Kit. Truth is . . . the word is, it isn't just Hollows coming for him. Something worse."

Kit went cold even as she drank in another gulp of hot tea. *What could be worse than Hollow Men?*

"You can stay here for a little time," said Ash. "Rest

for an hour or two. Even for you, today must have been tiring. But after that, I'll wake you and you leave. And you run. Can you do that?"

Kit stared into her tea. Her head tipped forward, short locks falling around her face. A dark reflection stared back at her, tired and wild-eyed. Scared.

"Run away. Survive. Live. Can you do it, Kit?"

"Of course. That's what I'm good at."

Lord Doyle grimaced behind the glass of his steam coach. Although he was in charge of running Industrial, he did not like coming here. The place was bad for a man's health, as could be seen on the faces of those who lived here. That, and these people hated him.

Thankfully, few people walked the streets tonight — the sight of filthy, starving mongrels made his stomach turn. Even the street itself offended him, the cobbles jarring his coach up and down much more than in other districts.

The machine slowed, exhausting steam into the air with

a ghostly whine. A servant opened the door and Doyle waddled his way out of the vehicle, cursing when his fine shoes plopped into a foul-smelling puddle. "Circle the area," he grumbled. "I won't be long."

The driver nodded and the coach rolled away, quickly disappearing into a blend of factory smoke, phosphorescent green light, and its own steam trails.

Doyle scanned the streets, grunting when he was satisfied no one was waiting in the shadows to slit his throat. He resisted the urge to brandish his pistol, instead walking forward. Two pairs of red eyes glowed in the distance, watching him approach. When he was close enough, he could see the Callidus Hollows' faces, the dim light catching their skull-like features.

"The boy, he's here, isn't he?" demanded Doyle. One of the Hollows snarled at him. "I'll hope that was a yes," he mumbled.

A short gust of wind broke through the humid, smoky air, and Doyle's blood froze. There, in the green pool of light to his left, stood Bell Begor and Mr. Zeb. Zeb drew deep on his aged, oscuro cigar, looking amused.

"Devils abound! Lord Doyle. I never expected to see you on these streets. What are you doing here?"

"I've been tracking the boy's movements," the noble answered, trying to sound gruff. "Given that this is Ash's place, I presume you've come to the same conclusion?"

"Excellent deduction. See, Bell, our lord still has his wits about him, no matter what O'Toole says." Mr. Zeb released another puff from his thickly-wrapped cigar, a hellish-orange glow reflecting in Mr. Zeb's soft, luminescent eyes. Begor simply watched her lord, bored.

"Well? Shall we?" Doyle grew uncomfortable among Industrial's nighttime world, especially with the two Hollows watching in the shadows. The presence of the attendants didn't help his feelings at all.

Mr. Zeb knocked on the door. A smiling pair of eyes looked through the hole, saw Zeb, and grew scared. The door opened quickly, and a younger brothel girl shielded herself behind the heavy door, gesturing them in. Doyle could tell the girl knew both Zeb and Begor, and not in a good way.

"After you, my lord" insisted Mr. Zeb. "After all, it is

your head on the chopping block."

Doyle frowned at the attendant, then stepped into the wanton Rusted Rose.

Having not dozed off yet, Kit sat up as she heard footsteps running up and down the hall outside her room. She jumped out of bed and went to see what the commotion was. Ash was giving directions to some of her girls.

"What's happened?" asked Kit walking toward them.

"Kit!" exclaimed Ash. "You need to get out. Or maybe just hide in your room."

"Hide from what? What aren't you telling me?"

The girls looked between Ash and Kit. Their mistress waved a hand, and they scattered.

The truth hit Kit like a wall, even though it was what she'd been expecting "They've come for him, haven't they?"

"It doesn't matter to you! You have to leave. Now."

Kit threw her cape around her shoulders, cinching it.

"I can't let it happen."

"Can't let . . . This is not your business. I'm telling you now, get gone!"

Kit took a deep breath and nodded, walking past her friend. Ash's hand stopped her, gently resting on her shoulder. "Please. Listen to me on this. Leave him. Save your skin, girl."

Kit shook her head. "No."

"Of all of the times to grow feelings. Don't do it! You'll regret it."

Ignoring Ash's warnings, Kit walked to Lukos' door, banging on it.

The two women stood awkwardly in the small hallway, staring at each other, a decent distance now between them.

The door opened, drawing Kit's attention. Lukos, eyes bloodshot and thick with sleep, appeared, disoriented, having awoken sharply at the abrupt knocking. Much like Kit, he was dressed from head to toe the same as before, looking slightly more rumpled from sleep.

"What?" he asked blearily. "Is something wrong?"

"We need to get out of here. They've found us."

Lukos nodded several times before marching forward. "Thank you for letting us rest here," he told Ash. "I know it must have brought you danger and such."

Ash gave Kit an apologetic glance, shaking her head. Her hand snaked out as Lukos passed, grabbing his left arm in a stone grip. She gave him the same sad look. "I'm sorry, Lukos, but I can't let you leave."

"Ash, what are you doing?" asked Kit. "What's going on?"

"Kit, love. You have got to run. This is the last time I'm going to say it."

Voices began spilling in from the backstage changing area—new voices, two men and a woman.

"Lord Doyle," said Lukos. "I know that voice." He struggled anew against Ash.

"Leave!" pleaded the brothel owner, pushing at Kit still.

The young thief shook her head. "This isn't like you! You help people like him, not the nobles."

"Kit, please, girl—"

"No! Not until I know what's going on."

Taking advantage of their indecision, Lukos pulled

away, twisting his arm from Ash's grip. Before he could get far, he felt her hand steady and firm at his neck.

"Let go," he said, struggling to breathe. "I don't want to hurt you."

She laughed. "You wouldn't be able to. Even with that metal arm of yours."

From where she stood, Kit watched Lukos' eyes panic. She grabbed a small piece of paneling leaning against a wall and slammed it against Ash's back. The brothel owner let Lukos go, momentarily shocked.

"Run, Lukos!"

As the voices from the front room grew louder, Ash turned to Kit with a confused, sorrowful look.

"I'm sorry," said Kit. "But I can't be the only one to get away this time. There's something about him that's right, when everything else in this town is so wrong."

She wasn't surprised when Ash reached for her, even if a little hurt. Friends turn on each other after enough time—for Kit, that was just a fact of life. And being so, she had expected some form of retaliation. What she didn't expect was Ash's eyes to flicker with a fiery glow.

Already on the defensive, Kit dodged her, but froze when she saw Ash's eyes. "What *are* you?"

"I tried to warn you."

Ducking under another grab, Kit threw the paneling into her face, running after Lukos. Kit saw two men burst through the beaded doorway from the corner of her eye as she turned the corner of the hallway. She quickly caught up with a lost and hesitating Lukos, yelling at him, "This way!" as angry voices gave chase.

Kit made a sharp turn, nearly pummeling into the wall where a vent sat loosely on its hinges. She lifted the metal, pushing Lukos into the cramped airspace. The voices grew close.

"Hurry. They're almost here."

Lukos slipped inside enough for Kit to follow, just as she glimpsed Ash's blue heels at the end of the hall. She urged him forward. "She'll know we're here. Move faster."

Lukos mumbled some form of acknowledgement in the dark, squeezing forward on his elbows and knees as the ventilation system grew consistently narrower. Something solid crashed into the wall, ripping apart the vent and clawing chunks out of the duct. Kit looked back on hands and knees, watching as a woman in an indigo dress with a white collar tried to force and tear her way into the ventilation shaft, her apathetic face not matching her rapid, vicious movements. The woman was fast, but her frame too large.

Kit took a breath and kept moving forward, telling Lukos to take a left.

Sneaking a last peak before she followed him around the corner, Kit saw blue eyes glowing in the dark. The woman snarled at them and pulled herself from the duct at an inhuman speed. Kit stared at the empty space for a small eternity before finding the strength to move again.

Bell Begor ripped herself from the wall, creating a web of cracks and causing Doyle to jump.

"She's leading him through the vents," said Ash. "I've laid the system out in a complicated network of escape tunnels, for the girls."

"Have you now?" hissed Mr. Zeb. "That's wonderful, Ash. I'm glad you have escape routes all figured out for your whores. Maybe next time you can simply escort our enemies through the front door!"

Mr. Zeb and Ash stared each other down in the hallway. Bell Begor stepped between them, her usual lack of expression tinged with impatience.

"We are wasting time. Where will they get out?"

Ash waved the two attendants aside. "Hard to say. The system runs throughout the entire building, but if I were Kit, I would want to get to the street. That's where she's comfortable. And there are only two vents that lead out."

Mr. Zeb leaned against the wall, his top hat in hand, thinking. "This girl, is she clever or just another one of your employees?"

"She's a thief, and a damn good one at that."

"Then, knowing you are with us now, she will be expecting us at those two exits. You and Doyle will go to the two exit vents. Tell me any other likely places that she would lead him and Bell and I will stand by at those."

"Shouldn't one of us stay here, just to make sure they

won't double back?"

"No," he said, giving her a sociopathic smile. He grabbed some bank notes, bills, and a book of matches from his jacket pocket. Zeb dropped the paper in front of the air ducts and, with a sudden cruel gleam in his eye, stuffed the matchbook back into his jacket. "Because, Ash, you are going to smoke them out."

"You want me to start a fire in my own house?"

"The sooner the better."

"No."

Mr. Zeb cocked an eyebrow. "Excuse me?"

"I said, no." Ash crossed her arms.

"I command you to light it!" he shouted, finger jabbing at the wall.

"We are equals, Zeb. I am not your subject."

Mr. Zeb let his hand fall slowly, and stepped forward. Nose-to-nose, they stood fighting an unseen battle of will and fury. "Perhaps you are not beneath my rule, but do not forget who I am in Mr. Lucy's absence."

"I won't do it," she persisted, although her voice began to falter. "I'm not going to risk burning down —"

"Would you risk throwing away all of our time and effort, then?"

A terrible silence held the hallway captive and Ash's eyes flared red again. Without ceasing to glare at her self-claimed superior, she waved a hand at the open duct. There was a pop, and the notes and papers began to smolder. Doyle tried to look away, wiping the nervous sweat from his brow.

Mr. Zeb patted her on the shoulder. "Good girl. Now, Miss Bell, shall we go and receive our young charge?"

A lazy fan spun underneath Lukos. Four other ducts continued over it. "It splits off, here, right, left, up, onward—"

"I know what it does," Kit snapped. She paused, seeming to think for a minute. Lukos decided it would be best not to interrupt her. "Take the one going left."

Not arguing, Lukos did as he was told, carefully balancing and bending over the spinning fan as he went.

"Where does it lead?" he asked.

"Just keep going, would you? This isn't a time to talk."

He clamped his mouth shut and scooted forward, cursing his own slow progress. A sound caught his ear, and he stopped to listen.

An impatient growl came from behind him.

"Did you hear that?"

"No, now go!"

A few paces later, he thought he heard the sound again, and now he could smell something. *A dead rat, maybe?* Too bitter, and somewhat sweet.

"There it is again. What is that?"

In place of an answer, Kit's breathing grew deeper behind him, more frantic. Then he got a good whiff of it—it clouded his vision and sent pain through his head. Smoke. The sound grew louder behind them. It was crackling, and underneath, a growing roar of fire.

A voice drifted through the system, unnaturally loud and clear. It held a deep and playful tenor, sinister in its amiable tone. *"Come out, Lukos! You can't hide in there forever. We have a new world to build."*

"Lukos," said Kit calmly. Too nicely. "You have to go

faster. Don't breathe when you can handle it, just move."

He nodded in the darkness, digging his left fingers into the thin metal around him. A buzzing filled their senses, and flies swarmed them in the dark. Spurred on by both disgust and fear, Lukos propelled himself forward as best as he could manage, conserving his breath.

The voice didn't return, and the flies died down, at the cost of a quickly thickening smoke. Lukos thought the air system would have been able to filter the polluted air faster, but it only seemed to speed it along, more every second. It became unbearable, an extreme from which Lukos was unable to keep his eyes open for the sting.

Asphyxia began its painful assault, steadily grabbing hold of Lukos' lungs, and then his arms and legs. It was only when Kit pushed him forward from behind that he realized he had stopped moving. He coughed horribly and slid on his hands and knees, bumping into something.

It was sharp, uncomfortable, and cold, and Lukos could feel a gust of fresh air coursing through it. His eyes snapped open, watering, stinging, blurring immediately. Kit pushed him again, not realizing they'd reached the grate.

Lukos slid his metal fingers through the slits and grasped firm, effortlessly bending the small gate. With a hard push, the entire frame was ripped away from its screws.

Lukos crawled forward, falling headfirst onto a cobblestoned alley behind the Rusted Rose. Kit toppled out behind him directly, allowing herself to cough and suck in a gulp of air.

"Well, that . . . was horrid," she rasped.

Lukos nodded, coughing out watery mucus and smoke-black phlegm.

Kit stood slowly, avoiding the open vent, which was now billowing smoke. "Ash designed the ventilation system. It won't take her long to figure out where we came out."

At the entrance to the alley, a man stepped in front of the green street light. His features were lit just enough for Lukos to see. The former servant felt a jolt of dread run through his body.

"Lukos," said the man, stern, coming into full view. "There you are."

"Who is that?" Kit whispered.

Lukos glanced over his shoulder and stood in front of

Kit. Her face was on a wanted poster because of him, but perhaps if they caught him, they would leave her alone.

"One of the nobles," he whispered back. "Lord Patterwicke Doyle. Keeper of Industries."

Chapter Four: A Guest for Dinner

"You've been a good servant, Lukos. Hardworking, resolute." Doyle took a step, his usual stiff, strict movements hindered by a nervous agitation. "Quite frankly, you're the best in staff. I would think that staying with me for another period of time would not be so bad."

Lukos' emotions boiled inside him, fear and his own paranoid nightmares bubbling to the surface. "Why are you doing this? Why go through all of this trouble for someone like me? I'm nothing."

Doyle's jaw worked, the Keeper of Industries trying to come up with a good answer.

"Does it have to do with the red room?" Lukos demanded. "Does it?"

"The red room . . . ?" Doyle let his question hang in

the air, sounding confused. But Lukos could see it in his eyes. Recognition.

"From when I was a child. Kneeling with other children, the room was dark." Lukos' voice shook, taking an involuntary step. "Someone led an animal in, a goat, I think. I remember how its blood felt when they cut its throat. Warm and thick. Tell me," he said, voice dangerous and low. "Why? What did it mean?"

Doyle's face scrunched in confusion. "There is no way you could recall that."

"What does it mean?" Lukos begged, his heart skipping a beat. "Why shouldn't I remember? What does it have to do with me?"

Doyle shook his head, and reached deep into his coat pocket. "It's all going to hell." He pulled out a small handgun and pointed it at Lukos. The old war veteran's tone sounded broken. "Nothing is happening as it should. I might as well end this misery and confusion for you—I'm sure the alchemists can keep you alive until everything is in motion."

Fear gripped Lukos, he tried to keep his mind and

emotions in check. He had survived the Hollows, he would survive this.

Kit jumped from behind him, throwing a cloud of glittering dust into the air, pulling Lukos to the ground. A gunshot pierced Industrial, and a hole swished through the dust cloud. Lukos cried out as the lead ball grazed his metal arm, ricocheting off at an odd angle.

They could hear Lord Doyle sputter a stream of curses. "Curse you! You have no idea what trouble you've caused!"

Kit growled from beneath Lukos, pushing him up. "Did you get hit?"

"I'll be fine," Lukos said, glad to know she cared.

"Get ready to run."

Lukos saw what she meant. Her glittery cloud was dissipating, Doyle's silhouette already taking aim. Lukos picked up the first thing his hand came across, the metal slats from the vent, and whirled them at Doyle. The sharp edges clipped the fat noble, causing the man to stumble back in surprise. The gun fired again, and this time Lukos felt like he'd been punched in the gut. Master and servant stared at each other with varying degrees of shock and fear.

Kit threw a brick at the noble, who dodged it. The distraction was long enough for Lukos to lunge forward, landing his left fist into Doyle's jaw. The noble sunk to the ground, unconscious, and Lukos ran, a sharp pain jabbing his side every time his feet met the road.

Kit caught up with him, surprised. "Are you okay?" She watched him warily, waiting for Lukos to reveal any wounds.

"I'm fine," Lukos gasped. In truth, his stomach flared with pain and emotions swirled within him that he had never felt. Rage, frustration, and hatred for the nobles sent streaks of heat throughout his body, rivaled only by confusion and desperation for knowing why his life had become a race against horrors.

"It's a kill or be killed world," Kit said, seeing the conflict written all over his face. "You did what you had to. You did less than most would have, to be honest."

Lukos shook his head, struggling with her statement.

They were back on the streets, and a small crowd had gathered in front of the Rusted Rose, pointing up as fires licked at the windows upstairs. Men and women tumbled out the front door, coughing and blind from the billowing smoke. Any of the Hollow Men that had been here earlier were nowhere in sight.

"Which way?" Lukos asked. His eye caught something in front of the Rusted Rose. "Oh, no."

Kit stepped up next to him, scanning every possible route of escape like a trapped animal. "What's wrong?"

Lukos didn't say. Emerging from the front door came a face he recognized—and one he was fearing more and more with each passing moment. From her place in the crowd Begor spotted him as well, and Lukos felt the weight of her focus suffocate him. She stepped toward the runaway and the pickpocket.

An explosion rocked the Rusted Rose. Accompanied by shouts and the scream of a single woman inside, the blast knocked the crowd back .like pins, sending out bits of glass, splintered wood, and copper shrapnel.

Daring to lower a protective hand from his eyes, Lukos saw Begor immediately. So close to the Rose, she'd been thrown several feet. Her legs were twisted like a rag doll, large shards of glass protruding out of her back, neck bent at the wrong angle.

And then she began to twitch, her head whipping forward, neck bones still poking under the skin where they shouldn't, legs and arms untangling slowly to push herself up into a standing position.

"Come on," urged Kit, "let's get out of here." She was still looking around, unknowing of Begor. Lukos clamped a hand over her mouth, dragging her into an alleyway. She bit his hand and punched furiously—pure reflex, he surmised. Lukos gritted his teeth, shushing her and finding safety a moment before Bell Begor's head twisted their way. Or at least, he hoped they had found safety.

Doyle's eyes flew open, giving him choice view of the muck he was laying in. Flames belched from the open vent in the Rusted Rose's side alley. He groaned, feeling the bruise already forming over his face. The young man fractured his jaw, he was sure of it. Either way, Doyle felt horrible after having met with the alley's hard ground.

Lukos was strong.

Lukos! Oh dear God, if you still exist, let him be here . . .
Doyle slipped twice, finally pushing himself up to his knees and crawling away from the alley, which grew hotter by the second. His eyes searched the streets, now more chaotic as people ran to and fro to keep the fire secluded to the Rusted Rose. The servant and his accomplice were gone.

"You had him," whispered Mr. Zeb, standing behind him. "Didn't you?"

Doyle fell over in panic, terror clutching his heart. He leered at the attendant's face, partially silhouetted in the torching glow of the fire. Zeb's eyes danced with a hellish light of their own.

"I-I-I'm sorry," sputtered Doyle, falling back on his hands. "My lord, it won't happen again."

Mr. Zeb leaned forward, his gloved hands clutching the noble's shoulders. "Again, Lord Doyle, that is a title unbefitting of me. I am your humble servant." Zeb pulled the rotund master to his feet, fingers gripping Doyle's arms too tightly. Despite his amiable tone, there was murder in the air mixing with the smoke from the fire.

Bell appeared before them. She was ghastly, with bits of debris sticking out of her back and head, skin protruding where bones and vertebrae had been misplaced. Her head sat crooked, scanning the alleyway now lined with small tongues of flame.

"Lukos was here," said Doyle. "I'm sure he ran that way! If we search for him, perhaps—"

Bell vanished, moving at an unholy speed. Mr. Zeb hushed the noble. "I'm afraid it is too late for that, now. The thief who accompanies him seems to be a competent survivor, and they are long gone. Your window of opportunity has closed."

"But I can fix it," pleaded the usually gruff Doyle.

Mr. Zeb laughed it off. "You sound so stricken, Lord Doyle. Don't worry so. I'm sure O'Toole will want to punish you," he said, his voice dropping in pitch for the completion of his statement, "but perhaps we can convince him otherwise over dinner? Find some other way to escape his wrath."

Doyle swallowed, nervous. "Dinner?"

"Yes. My treat. The three of us, dreaming of plans for

the future. Like old times." Begor returned, causing Mr. Zeb to sigh in exasperation. "What is it?"

"They've gone into hiding again. I'll send out the Igna-vus Hollow Men——"

"No, don't. The thief with Lukos is good at what she does. According to Ash, she's a pupil of Tom Vix."

A mix of shock and anger played over Doyle's features.

"Sending out more Hollows will only make her crawl deeper into hiding," Mr. Zeb continued. "No, get Mammon. He was in the Business District last. Tell him her name is Kit——a street thief with red hair, or black if she's wearing her usual disguise. He'll enjoy a good hunt."

Bell nodded once and was gone, leaving Mr. Zeb and Doyle alone.

"Bell Begor and Mammon are serious people. Efficient. I would say they are more than capable of tracking down our dear Lukos and this troublesome girl. Wouldn't you?"

Doyle nodded, in no position to question anyone.

"Well then," said Zeb. "I'm afraid I can't offer you my cab, as I walked here."

Doyle shook his head, still nervous but feeling relieved.

"I have my man circling the block. It may be difficult to reach him with this crowd, but we need only wait for him to come back around."

Mr. Zeb looked off into the swirl of smoke and fire. Amidst the crowd, Ash stopped coordinating the people trying to fight the fire long enough to glare at him. Mr. Zeb smiled at her. "Perfect, Lord Doyle, simply perfect."

Kit watched from her position under the grate leading into an aqueduct, nearly gasping at the impossible speed of the tall woman, as well as the debris jutting from her skin at all angles. She was glad Lukos was down below. If she had almost gasped, he certainly would have, and then they would both be done in. His breathing was already loud enough.

The woman turned, sniffing the air. She lingered for a moment, and Kit thought they would be outed. But the strange woman leapt to one of the larger rubbish bins, overturning it as if it were made of paper. Rubbish and scrap metal — pieces of iron, nickel, and copper to be recycled later — slid out, creating a great ruckus that hid the small clang Kit's frightened jump made against the ladder.

Above, the maid woman looked around again, as if she knew she was missing a vital clue. Kit was for once glad that there was so much grime and ash in Industrial — it made the grate invisible. As quickly as she had come, the woman disappeared, so fast that Kit hardly realized it.

Who was that? No, what was that? It was almost as bad as any Hollow Man, yet flesh and blood.

She looked below, unable to see Lukos in the dark. "Hurry and get onto the ladder!"

A pause in the darkness. Lukos' shifting feet created ripples. "Wait, are we going back up?" he rasped.

"Yes."

"But they're up there, aren't they? That was the whole reason we came down into this stinking hole. Because it wasn't safe up there."

"Down here's even worse, if you stay long enough."

Proving her point, the sound of metal on brick walls screeched at them from deep within the aqueduct. They both became deathly still, listening as something moved in the water, coming closer. Whatever it was grew distant again, moving toward a farther tunnel.

"Look," Kit said, "when you shoved me into a dead end, this was the only place we could hide until they passed. They passed." She hesitated. "Good work, by the way."

Looking down, she saw Lukos smile at the compliment, though his face was pale and sweaty, and more than from mere exhaustion or stress. Something was wrong.

"They might still be up there," he argued.

Kit sighed. "My survival instinct—a very strong instinct, by the way—tells me they've passed and moved on to the next step in finding us. That woman was moving faster than I could dream of. She'll be long gone now."

Lukos mumbled something about, "If you're sure." A moment later, Kit heard the thick soles of his boots thud against the rusty iron bars.

"I suppose that's it then," he said.

Kit slowly lifted enough of an opening in the grate to move through. "What's it?"

"The Hollow Men are everywhere, looking for me. Ash,

Doyle, even Miss Begor, all working like lunatics to find us. You were right, and I was wrong. So terribly wrong."

His voice shook, his emotions threatening to snap. Kit felt her heart break a little at the sound and admonished herself for the sentiment. *He's so good-natured. Stupid, honest, foolish good nature. He'll get himself killed!*

"It won't be long until they find me again," he continued, "and more people will die in their wake. I should have listened before. There's nothing I can do but give myself up."

"Now hold on, I don't plan on marching up to no one and—wait, what did you say?"

"I said . . . I will go and give myself up. I've caused enough trouble for you with Ash. I'm sorry. I know she was your friend. Maybe if I leave now . . ."

Lukos kept listing all of the reasons he could not put her in any more danger, but Kit was only half listening as he leaned against the dirty rungs. ". . . I think if they have me, they will forget about you. You can go back to—"

"Lukos, what's wrong? You're in pain." She screamed internally at herself for stopping him. He had just offered her the way out.

He stared at the brick wall. "I'm fine."

"Lukos, look at me!"

He looked up and started to fall. Moving quickly, Kit grabbed the front of his shirt, which was tacky with blood. It didn't take her long to understand.

"He did shoot you. Brickit, why didn't you tell me?"

Lukos shrugged. "We had other things to worry about."

She growled, dragging him up the ladder. "Do you realize what kind of trouble you're putting me through because you decided there were other things to worry about? This, we should have been worried about. Bricks, if any of that sewage got near your wound . . . From now on, you look out for yourself. Do you understand?" She pushed the grate open with some effort, and then dragged Lukos out. "You keep on thinking about everyone else, you will die, Lukos. So stop it. Take care of yourself first, and that means telling me when you've been shot!"

Lukos struggled to climb up through the hole. "Are you crying?"

"No." She pulled him behind another trash bin — one

that hadn't been tossed around by some monster maid. "Wait here."

Lukos didn't argue. She was glad to see he had at least been putting pressure on the wound.

Kit ran off, blending with the shadows. Moments after, Lukos heard glass shatter. He waited, patient, worried, but also fearful enough to listen to her command. In her absence, Lukos noticed a few other figures darting about in the dark. It was late, and the only people out seemed to be children, which he presumed to be other thieves, or roguish men and women. He tucked himself closer into his sheltered crevice.

A woman ducked into the alley, and Lukos prepared to defend himself.

"Relax, it's me," said Kit, discarding a coat several times too big for her. She took different items from her large pockets.

"That was fast. Where did you get those?"

"Don't worry about it. This will hurt. Lift your shirt."

Lukos grimaced, peeling his shirt away from the wound.

"Good. It's just a flesh wound."

"You . . ." Lukos took a breath as she dabbed at the ruptured skin. "You call that a flesh wound?"

Kit glared, failing to warn him when she poured an unmarked and alcoholic bottle of what felt like liquid fire into the wound. He screamed, and she stuffed part of her sleeve into his mouth. "Be quiet! Of all the times to attract attention!"

A muffled *sorry* came through her sleeve.

"Bricks, you're such a baby. This next part's not so bad. Still, keep your mouth shut."

Lukos rolled up his own sleeve, gritting his teeth around it. He squeezed his pocket watch and closed his eyes, not wanting to know what was about to happen. Kit reached around his sides, wrapping him in fabric for makeshift bandages. Realizing he was okay, Lukos opened his eyes.

"I can only hope we're treating this in time. Where we're going, they'll have someone who is better at playing doctor take another look. I've packed this pretty well, but make sure you keep pressure on it. The worst of the bleeding should be over, but I don't want to be worrying about any more of your insides spilling."

Lukos exhaled slowly, afraid to move as she finished wrapping the gunshot wound. "Where are we going next? You have a plan?"

"Of course I have a plan. Didn't survive Industrial by flashing gold coins around." She smiled at him, even if just a little. "How do you feel?"

"Hellish. Hungry and sick at the same time. Tired." He looked it, too, pale and sickly, worn, an innocent soul who had shed the skin of boyhood completely in the span of a single birthday. "Why are you doing this for me? No offense, but you don't seem the type to take in helpless, and you don't even know me."

"When the Hollows found us in the Arts District, they were after you. I tried to pull you out of that building, but you told me to run, and then dropped yourself down in the midst of them. Why?"

Lukos shrugged. "It seemed the right thing to do. I knew if they caught you, you would be hanged."

Kit sat back, considering for a moment. "It's not to do the right thing. I'm not sure why I'm helping you." She stared out of the alley as a restful silence fell over them.

"Well, whatever reason you come up with, thank you. I'm not sure what I would've done without you."

"Died."

Lukos raised his eyebrows and nodded in agreement. "So? This place. Where is it?"

Kit looked beyond the alley, to the nearly empty streets, the friendly moment gone. "The Fox Den. I hadn't planned on going back, but we're out of choices. I just hope they let me back in."

Doyle lifted the silver to his mouth, pulling the meat from the fork with eager teeth. He allowed himself to melt from the sheer pleasure of the taste, the aroma, how the morsel comforted him — chewing slow at first. "This is delectable! At once, satisfying, and wholly exquisite."

"Roast mutton," Mr. Zeb flourished, "provided by my

personal favorite bioalchemist, and cooked to perfection by my chef."

"It's a perfect dish, Zeb, my compliments to your choice of chef. Given how quiet your mansion is, I almost thought your servant staff went missing."

The house had been deathly quiet when they entered, its expensive but drab décor flickering in cold firelight. It was more like some architect's intoxicated concept sketch than a place that had been lived in. The strange statues and depictions of insectoid grotesques did not help the alienating atmosphere. No one had arrived to take their coats, which Lord Doyle thought odd, especially when he heard thuds in the walls.

Mr. Zeb waved his hands. "Oh, don't misunderstand. I'm merely O'Toole's attendant, after all. I only require my chef."

"That cannot be true. With all of your—what did you call it, Gothic architecture? How on earth do you keep it all tidy?"

"Ah, yes. I admit, I have a weakness for such Pre-Destruction styles, and it can be too intricate too handle

sometimes. But really, other than my chef, I have no servants."

From somewhere in the house, Doyle heard something
like a crash, followed by the chirping of insects, buzzing
wings, skittering feet, rattling—

Mr. Zeb snapped his fingers and all fell silent but for
the crackling fireplace. "At least, no man servants," he said
with a chuckle. He waved a hand at Doyle's food. "Please,
eat. There is plenty more on its way from the kitchen."

Doyle resisted the urge to shiver. "When did Shekelton
say he would arrive?" He pulled at his collar, which had
begun to grip his thick neck too tightly.

"O'Toole? Who knows when that man decides to do
things? He will show shortly, but don't let that stop you
from eating."

For the first time since sitting down to the table, Doyle
set his fork down and sat back. He had consumed three
plates in the short time since he'd arrived, each a different
dish made to perfection. So busy was he devouring the
delicacies, Doyle hadn't noticed that Mr. Zeb neglected
his own meal. Rumors of the man's appetite—his nightly

prowls through Industrial — came to mind.

The attendant studied him coldly. "Something amiss, old boy?"

"Not at all, Zeb! As I said, this banquet is to die for! It's been a long day. It's rude of me, but I feel horrible all of the sudden and should rest." He started to stand. "Let me not disturb your abode any longer."

"Nonsense. I understand your plight. Lukos falls on your head. That is part of the reason I arranged this meeting, so that we might ease O'Toole's punishment."

Doyle laid his napkin on the table. "Much appreciated, Mr. Zeb. Still, I think I should —"

"I don't think you understand." Mr. Zeb appeared at Doyle's shoulder, which was impossible as the man had just been sitting at the far end of the table. Still, there he was, forcing Doyle back into his seat. "Stay. I insist. Here, let me pour you more wine."

Doyle's nervousness turned to fear, growing as he watched the blood-red wine spill into his glass. Mr. Zeb remained at his side.

"Please, Lord Doyle, drink. Eat. Be merry! Very soon,

you will not have to worry about your blunder with Lukos."

"I-I think I've had enough, thank you."

Mr. Zeb's grip tightened over the noble's shoulder. The attendant grabbed the abandoned silver fork and stabbed it into a mound of breaded stuffing. "Eat!"

"I've heard what you do in your spare time," Doyle said, a hint of disgust in his voice. "How you use Industrial as a hunting ground. You're a parasite. O'Toole might have needed you to win the war, but our alchemists will unlock the secret of immortality soon, without you or your Mr. Lucy. Very soon, we won't need you anymore."

"That's funny. I was thinking the same thing." Mr. Zeb picked up the fork and thrust it into Lord Doyle's face. The noble screamed as blood flowed from his cheek.

"Bastard! What are you doing? You forget your place!"

A fist slammed through Doyle's nose, crushing it.

"Not so. My contract is with Shekelton O'Toole, not with you. Foolish man, you should have never let your charge from your sight. I knew Begor's influence would be too powerful for your simple mind. Now open up."

Mr. Zeb proceeded to pry the noble's mouth open. The

two men struggled for a moment, but Zeb's violence was greater. He pulled the fork from Doyle's cheek, punching it twice more into Doyle's face, and then his neck. The injuries were painful, immobilizing, but nothing lethal.

In shock and knowing he was no threat to the attendant, Doyle held still as Mr. Zeb took the glass of wine and held it to the noble's lips. His words distorted by pain and a shattered nose, Doyle stared in horror and asked, "Why are you doing this?"

"Shush. Drink." Mr. Zeb titled the wine glass, satisfied when the Keeper of Industries swallowed it down. He then yanked the fork from Doyle's neck and scooped up some of the stuffing, shoveling it into the man's mouth. "Eat!"

Again, the noble did at he was told, grimacing when Zeb took hold of his jaw and moved it up and down.

"All of the things you people put stock into," Zeb murmured as he continued to force feed Lord Doyle. "Money, art, entertainment. It fascinates me, that you lower lifeforms would aspire to our height. All you really need is air, food, sex, sleep. But no, you try and become something you are simply not." Mr. Zeb's grin split his face in two.

"I love watching you try so hard. In all honesty, though, I have to thank you for your creativity with food. Only man could elevate gluttony to something akin to art."

Doyle felt worse with every successive morsel. His stomach felt like it was about to burst. He couldn't tell if it was bile in his throat, or if he was truly swallowing the food anymore. Speech felt impossible, but he managed to squeeze it out through short gurgling moans. "You vile thing. You're . . . the pretender here . . . not me."

Zeb frowned. "Now who's forgetting their place?"

"Rot in hell."

"'Tis better to rule in Hell than to serve in Heaven." Mr. Zeb grabbed the knife from Doyle's plate and pushed it into his shoulder, forcing a groan from the man. Then he dragged the Keeper of Industries out of his chair, toward the fireplace. With a final heave, Mr. Zeb threw Lord Doyle into the flames, an arm breaking over the metal grate's spikes.

"Stuffed and piping hot," Mr. Zeb said, his voice rising over Doyle's screams, "just the way I like them!"

Doyle rolled out of the fireplace, trying to escape. His

face and hands were already blistering. He threw unintelligible curses at the attendant, vocal chords shot. Mr. Zeb yanked the knife and fork from the Keeper of Industries and with a smooth motion ripped the man's neck open. A simple push sent him tumbling further back into the fireplace.

As Doyle's gurgles grew faint, the house came to life with the sounds of pestilence, the mad chorus of humming wings and dry slithering mixed well, otherworldly, with the crackle of the flame. Mr. Zeb licked the blood off one of his fingers, and then sat down. He held the fork and knife eagerly, watching, waiting for his evening meal to finish cooking.

Kit stopped walking and Lukos doubled over, glad for the moment's rest. He gulped for air, but the sudden heat sucked it all away from him. Lightheaded, he blinked away a minor dizzy spell and looked up to a large, dark building leaking red light and a loud clamor.

"Where are we?" he asked, after Kit closed the door behind him—all traces of cool or reasonably-moderate air shut out with it. Realizing she couldn't hear him over the din, he repeated the question, louder.

"One of the auto factories," she told him. Kit held a dirty handkerchief over her mouth and walked forward.

Lukos had heard about the factories—Lord Doyle owned most of them—but apparently his previous imaginings of simple assembly lines were inadequate.

The people of the Industrial District stood in too many lines from front to back, and on three separate levels of flooring and catwalks. Tables and conveyor belts and ugly panels with buttons and levers sprawled before them, with giant factory automatons towering in between them, monitoring every step. Dust danced through the air, a distasteful mix of dirt and oil covering every visible surface.

In the nearest line, Lukos watched as women sorted scraps of metal into iron bins and sent those bins down different conveyors. They were dispersed into several lines, some getting picked up by a central giant automaton with multiple hydraulic arms—probably driven by a small homunculus—which dumped the bins into large melting pots. Steam hissed from the automaton's joints, fires screeched against melting metal, and hammers and drills whirred and banged to create a conglomeration of sound that Lukos found deafening and disorienting.

He realized Kit was nowhere to be seen and panicked until he spotted her walking toward him between two lines of burly men hammering away at metal plates. With a roll of her eyes, she marched over and grabbed his jacket sleeve, turning back to continue her interrupted route. The men squinted at Lukos as they walked by, some with a frightened, manic look in their eyes. Kit tugged hard on his arm.

"Don't make eye contact," she whisper-yelled over her shoulder. "Remember, you're famous."

He glanced behind as one of the men left his station to grab a speaking tube from the wall. Lukos gulped, forcing his eyes forward.

As they pushed through the workroom—workers ignoring them, some yelling for them to get out if they weren't there to work—he got a better understanding of what she meant by an auto factory. At the far side of the room he could see several finished products like the steam carriages, and even two or three personal automobiles that people like the nobles used. Automaton servants hung from chains in different stages of completion. A man placed a wriggling homunculus in the chest of one finished automaton as Lukos watched, causing the metal shell to spring to life. The homunculus-driven machine was dropped from its chains and led into a smaller room that Lukos couldn't see.

Kit's hand on his arm jerked him to the right, and the lines of automobiles and automatons disappeared from his sight. Before them was a partitioned section inhabited by children. Lukos felt sick to his stomach, not just from the gunshot wound.

Wearing masks that were obviously not enough to protect them from the foul air, several dozen children sat at steel tables constructing automaton pets — cats, dogs, parakeets. Metallic friends to fit every lord and lady's fancy, designed after beasts that were all but mythology after the Great Destruction. To the side of the group was a moderately large furnace blazing fully. Lukos leaned up against a metal beam, perspiring from the heat.

Among the garden of focused, sweating children, eyes forward to their tasks, one popped up with giant, surprised eyes. Lukos could see Biggy smile through his rag of a face mask. Just as quickly, his smile fell and fear consumed his eyes.

They made their way through the groups of long tables.

"You shouldn't be here," Biggy urged Kit, looking over his shoulder twice.

Immediately, she was on alert. "What is it?"

"Hollows are here looking for you. Been making a proper run through all of Industrial, so I hears."

Lukos watched as Kit's terror visibly shook her. Watched as she forced it down.

"I'll get out of your hair quick, then. I need to get into the Fox Den."

"That's the problem, Kit."

Click, clack, click, clack, click, clack.

Kit shook her head, eyes trained on the ground below, only a few feet away. "No . . ."

Lukos followed her eyes and saw the metal grate in front of the furnace. He could hear something moving around down in the hole. And it was getting closer.

"It's like they knew exactly where to look," said Biggy. "They went right to it."

Kit bounced on her toes, looking around the area. "Ash! She must have told them. She's one of them, Biggy. You can't trust her anymore."

The boy looked heartbroken, his lip quivering, but she went on, speaking rapidly as the metal clicking grew louder and louder.

"I need to get to the Fox Den. Where is it right now?"

"You just missed them. They're moving to the Lake of Fire next."

A metal leg shot out of the hole. Kit shoved the boy back down to his table.

"Thanks, Biggy. Wait for them to pass, then run the hell out of here."

"I want to go with you."

"No! It's all too horrible, Biggy. Stay!"

Without another word, she sped off. Lukos saw several

other legs emerging from the hole. He didn't hesitate to do the same.

They ran the way they came, only some of the men from before were watching for them. With the Hollows inside the factory, Lukos now understood their wild, fearful expressions. A frail man in a dark suit was with one of them. He spotted them, then lifted a communicator to his mouth.

"This is bad," said Kit. "We're trapped!"

Confirming her observation, two Avidum Hollow Men appeared in the doorway they had entered. Factory workers scattered, opening a direct path between the two runaways and the Hollows.

"Kit!"

Lukos and Kit spun. Biggy waved at them frantically, both of his spindly arms crossing over his head.

"They're all around," he yelled at them. "You have to go up!" The boy didn't notice the two Avidum skittering from behind.

"Biggy, get away!"

One of the Avidum lifted its sharpened leg as Biggy

turned his head. He didn't move out of the way in time. The spider-like Hollow jabbed forward, and the limb appeared in the middle of Biggy's chest. The boy was lifted into the air, impaled.

Lukos had never felt such rage before. The building in the Arts District, all of those people dying under the ruin — it still haunted him. But Biggy was just a child. Beside him, Kit's wail gave voice to his own horror, but not to the fire that grew in his belly.

Biggy held stiff for a moment, then fell limp. The Avidum shook the small body off, as if Biggy were debris to be collected and recycled later.

"Monsters," yelled Lukos. He stepped forward, heat spreading from his shoulders all the way to his eyes, but something held him back. He looked over his shoulder, livid.

Kit was shaking her head at him. There were tears in her eyes, and he could see the same hatred he felt, brimming inside of her. Her fears became clear to him — this was not the first time she had lost someone. He looked at Biggy one last time, burning the image of the dead boy into his mind.

It wasn't cowardice that drove Lukos and Kit to run away. He hoped it was bravery in and of itself, a will to keep on living in this forsaken world. Chaos ensued. As runaway and thief ran, the Avidum began a steady scuttling forward, running anyone through that got in their way. Factory workers scrambled, dropping their duties and screaming to get away from the monstrous creatures. These were certainly not automatons. Hollow Men were behind them and Hollow Men filled in front of them as well. Lukos was sure if he kept looking, they would be flanked by them too.

Kit had to pull him along. The pain in his side was becoming more intense, and the harsh environment sapped energy that he didn't have to begin with. She led him to a frail looking ladder and made sure he could hold onto the rungs without passing out.

Up, Biggy had said. People streamed down the rungs, but it was their only immediate avenue to the next floor. Kit fought her way up, crawling on the back and the side of the ladder to pass the workers fleeing down. Lukos followed the best he could, crying out only once when someone crushed his fingers underfoot. He learned to hold the ladder differently, determination setting in.

Below, he saw the Hollows looking up with their blank, empty eyes. Like in the Arts District, they couldn't go up the ladder.

Instead, they tore it down.

Lukos was at the top rung when the ladder gave way. He grabbed the metal catwalk with his left hand, fingers crunching into the metal walkway. Kit pulled him up the rest of the way as people fell and clung for their lives beside them. The ladder smashed to the bottom floor with a horrible racket, landing on workers and work tables alike. Ruined metal soon clogged the assembly lines, causing sparks to fly, and smoke began to drift upward as the control panel of a conveyor belt was destroyed. The machines kicked into high gear, no longer regulated.

Kit dragged Lukos to his feet, immediately taking to a run again. The fugitive servant stopped to help the dangling workers.

"Leave them!" she called back.

"I won't!"

Growling, Kit charged back. Together, they pulled up the last of the factory workers, and before Lukos could inhale a deep breath Kit shoved him forward. Pushing their way through the crowded second floor, they came to another ladder.

"Where are we going?" he called to her as they began climbing.

"I have an idea."

Lukos looked down to the bottom floor, trying to find the Hollows. After a moment of not being able to see them, he noticed movement at a far wall. The Hollows were climbing.

There, on one of the giant arms of the factory automatons, stood a tall man in a pinstriped suit wearing green spectacles. Lukos watched, bewildered, as the man rode the mechanical arm up to the second floor. He casually stepped off onto the second floor catwalk. The man nodded, tipping his hat.

This man, Lukos knew, was like Begor and Ash. However, there was something . . . else . . . about him. The whole of the catwalk began to shake and tremble as the Avidum reached the structure.

Lukos clambered after Kit.

Neither of them spoke as they ran across the third floor bridge, a sooty stretch of metal hanging between two huge cylinders that smoked and glowed with molten metal. This upper level had become empty of other bodies, leaving them no cover as the factory workers ran for their lives below. They reached a crossway with another bridge at the same time something below exploded. Smoke and dust reached the ceiling in a rapid-expanding mushroom cloud. The floor tilted, throwing them into the side rail.

Lukos gasped, feeling the hole in his side stretch too far. The catwalk continued to rattle, bringing him back to the immediate threat. "We don't have much time!"

That was when the man with the green spectacles climbed up the side of the catwalks, and jumped over the railing to stand before them.

Chapter Five: Those, Underground

Shekelton O'Toole stormed through Mr. Zeb's dreary mansion, ignoring the way the shadows seemed to hum and flicker in the corners of his eyes. His silver snake ring clicked against his cane in rhythm with each furious step.

Spending the evening pacing back and forth over his office rug had proved frustrating enough before he received word that the Rusted Rose had burned to the ground. Receiving the message from Mr. Zeb was the fiery straw that set the camel aflame.

Preposterous, thought O'Toole, *him, summoning me! The audacious . . . I am not the servant.*

It had been years since Limbo's governing head had taken a step in Mr. Zeb's abode. He held an intense dislike for his attendant and spent as little time as possible around the man. The mansion, with all its empty personality and eerie, sharply made furnishings didn't soothe O'Toole's unease.

He saw the large black doors, inscribed with their obscene fly-like creature, and the hollow light that poured out onto the dusty floor. *The dining room, of course*, thought O'Toole, *you vile thing*. He quickly became aware of the revolting smell of charring flesh and steeled himself for the worst.

With as much anger as he could muster, he threw the doors wide, sending a loud *bang* through the vaulted ceilings and long hallways. Mr. Zeb sat near the middle of the table, his back to the fireplace, looking unsurprised. "Lord O'Toole! So good of you to come. I'm afraid you've just missed Lord Doyle, however. The poor man insisted on leaving."

O'Toole raised a finger, ready to unleash every complaint and frustration he'd thought of that night upon his attendant. He froze in his tracks, seeing the blood on Zeb's hands and face, and the trail of smudged crimson that led from the table to . . .

His eyes fell on the fireplace, pupils constricting. O'Toole slowly looked from the decapitated body that sat in the firebox, still burning, back to Mr. Zeb.

He saw the head that sat on a plate before him — skull cut open to reveal the gray matter inside. Mr. Zeb casually sliced a strip of the stuff out, and properly, with discerning manners, lifted it to his mouth, sucking it from the fork. It was Doyle, the brutalized face hardly recognizable.

"I did try to keep him here until you showed," Mr. Zeb continued, "but he just wouldn't hear of it."

Shekelton O'Toole walked forward. Each footfall was slow, steady. Dangerous. "You monster. I gave . . . no . . . order . . . whatsoever. To touch Doyle. Much less . . ."

"My lord, the man was incompetent. I warned you that living so close to Bell Begor would have an effect on him. Men grow lazy in her care."

"Dammit, Zeb! Patterwicke Doyle was not yours to have!" Watching his attendant take another nonchalant bite from Doyle's decapitated head, O'Toole shot forward several strides, grasping Mr. Zeb's neck.

Mr. Zeb froze, dropping his fork, which clattered

over his plate. Seeing a recognition of pain in Zeb's eyes, O'Toole squeezed, his silver ring cutting into the attendant's skin. It began to grow warm, a peal of smoke rising between them.

"You forget your place," growled the archduke. "I am your master. You are my servant. I give the order. You follow it, like the dog that you are." O'Toole released Mr. Zeb's neck, feeling satisfaction at the blistered burn his ring had left on the man's skin. "I'm tearing this godforsaken house to the ground. From now on, you will live in my mansion, learning how to become a proper attendant again. You will do as I say, and only as I say. And from now on, each . . . meal . . ." O'Toole shivered at the word, "will be brought to me for inspection. No more wild dog hunting in the streets. You will eat only who I allow you to, only the most vile and useless criminals in Limbo. Do I make myself clear?"

Mr. Zeb sighed, an infuriatingly relaxed sound. "You do, my lord."

"Do not test me, Zeb. We are close to our goal. The sooner we wake Mr. Lucy, the sooner you and I can be rid of each other."

"Spoken like a true leader of men." Mr. Zeb smiled at O'Toole. It was an amiable smile, no doubt holding back a tongue as sharp and murderous as a dagger.

O'Toole glanced at the fireplace, feeling his stomach turn. He felt a pang of loss in his gut, small flashbacks of fighting alongside Patterwicke Doyle assaulted his mind. The noble had been his friend and right-hand man at one time.

"Just one question," Mr. Zeb postured, breaking into his memories. "Before you go tearing down my house, may I finish my meal? I'm famished. Doyle turned out to have at least a little fight left in him."

O'Toole's nostrils flared, which only caused the horrid smell that filled his senses to grow worse. "Mammon is in Industrial. He's found Lukos. Go. Do your work. I will burn this place down myself." He muttered to himself, "Limbo's already seen one fire tonight, what's another?"

Mr. Zeb sighed again and folded his napkin. The attendant stood, gave a short bow, and walked out the door.

As O'Toole found a lantern and threw it to the ground,

Mr. Zeb allowed his face to split with a grin. He wished O'Toole had been more severe, but still the archduke's reaction served Mr. Zeb's purposes just fine.

It was time for him and Mammon to act.

Kit stopped in her tracks, a less nimble Lukos crashing into her from behind. On a good day, Kit would face off against any man over Hollows, but one look told her that this man was not a normal case. His striped suit was pristine, eyes completely hidden by those lenses, topped off with long white dreads, and he had just used a factory automaton as a makeshift staircase. A slick smirk told her that he was enjoying himself immensely. Not a normal resident of Industrial by any means, or Limbo, for that matter. He took a step forward.

"Back!" Kit hissed, and Lukos scurried to get out of the way. Turning their back on the strange man, the two ran back to the crossways between the bridges, now partially collapsed from the explosion. Three of the Avidum Hollows were already closing in from one of the suspended paths. Kit darted left without hesitation, redirecting her attention to a large bay window.

Behind her, Lukos screamed. Fighting years of instinct, Kit grasped the handrails to stop dead. She forced herself to turn around.

There was no way the man could have crossed the distance between them that quickly. Yet, there he was, holding Lukos in the air by the throat, his smiling eyes crinkling from behind those hideous spectacles. Kit's heart dropped.

"Good try!" the man praised Lukos. "Those narrow escapes today were dramatic and exciting. Well done, really. But you cannot truly hide from us in Limbo."

Lukos didn't respond, his face reddening deeper by the second. His attempted gasps for air were silent and empty.

Kit looked at the window, then back at the quickly approaching Hollows; at Lukos, then the window again. If she went back for him now, she would more than likely be killed. It was suicide.

Cursing herself, she charged, jumping into the man with all of her might.

It was like hitting a brick wall. Kit stumbled back, nursing her now-bruised shoulder as the man seemed to notice her for the first time. He grabbed Kit by the neck, lifting her from the catwalk, appraising her for a moment. He grew disinterested. She was unimportant, a thief; merely an accessory to Lukos, their true goal, who they needed alive.

By the increasing pressure around her neck, she guessed they didn't need her in the same condition.

Through fading vision, Kit watched her own helpless hands scratching at his arms. *No! Brick it all, I will not die here! I won't . . . can't . . .*

The tips of her fingers grew numb, the lack of feeling spreading to her mind. Her eyes fluttered closed.

A grunt roused Kit to her senses. She forced her eyes open again, in time to see Lukos grab the man's arm — with his metal hand. At first, the man didn't seem to think anything of it, until Lukos' fingers constricted. It was only then the strange man began to panic. In seconds, his forearm bent with a *pop*.

The spectacled man growled, dropping them both, and Kit felt the blood rush back through her neck. She sucked air into her lungs, crumpling onto the catwalk.

"Who are you?" Lukos cried, ignoring his raw throat. "What do you want?"

Kit was up now, pulling at Lukos' shoulder. She was only too aware of the sharp metal feet scuttling closer and closer over the trembling catwalks. "There's no time."

He shook her off. "Why are you looking for me?"

The man frowned at him. His face was a cross of pain and irritation. "You are the key to the new world, Lukos. You will restore the future. And me."

"I won't do a thing for you," Lukos rasped, pushing the man against the railing, threatening to push him over. His eyes were feral, scared. "Maybe I should just let you fall here. One less of you to deal with. That's how you work, isn't it? Kill whoever gets in your way? Those people in the shop? Biggy?"

Kit could see a darkness pour from Lukos. It was a desire for vengeance that she herself knew and had lived with her entire life. But seeing it in Lukos made her sick, frightened. Such an innocent soul, so suddenly filled with murderous intent. This was not the man she had come to know. "Lukos, don't . . ."

The spectacled man merely smiled as he was pushed farther over the edge. "You wouldn't. You are too tame. Besides, I won't let you. The world is depending on your clean hands, Lukos. Kill me now and condemn the world to an eternity of living in this present hell."

"Watch me!"

"No! Watch me." The man shoved Lukos back, nearly sending him flying. Kit caught him from behind. The well-dressed man ignored his mangled, loose limb and made for another grab at Lukos.

Lukos ducked and swung with a fast left hook, landing on the man's jaw. It was effective. He stumbled back, leaning too much on the handrails, which shifted.

Kit grabbed Lukos and pushed him forward. "Go!"

Looking over her shoulder only once, she watched the man tumble backward as the railing gave way. He fell out of sight, engulfed by the raging factory fire below and taking a chunk of the rails with him. Their catwalk started to shake.

The first Hollow was at the cross section, and she was

looking forward again.

"Where are we going?" Lukos yelled back.

It was a valid question. This particular section was a dead end, and the pounding of metal feet grew louder behind them, shaking the catwalk harder now.

Kit ducked by Lukos, passing him easily on the narrow path. She almost laughed at his terrified grumbling as he was pressed against the rail, her emotions brimming on hysteria. "Follow me!" If she was right, this was the bay window facing the south side of town. There should be a small roof on this side of the factory that they could land on and escape. One thing the spidery Hollow Men could not do — for which Kit was thankful — was jump. They were too heavy.

Lukos began to slow behind her, but she pressed on even faster, hoping he would get the hint. The window was fast approaching. Her gut clenching, Kit grabbed the guardrail and jumped.

Everything seemed quiet in mid air, without the Hollow Men's pounding feet resounding through her legs. Time seemed slower. Kit brought her arms and knees up as a shield, closing her eyes as she collided with the window. A shard of glass cut into her cheek.

The night air was muggy, but compared to being inside the burning factory it was frigid. Kit's eyes snapped open, and she prayed any shattered glass was far away. She heard Lukos cry out behind her, "Kit!" and looked beneath her feet, where the side roof should have been — if she had been correct.

Plummeting toward the hard street below, Kit realized she was wrong.

Lukos charged forward, telling himself to jump through the window. If Kit had done it, it had to be the right thing to do. *Right?* He grabbed the railing, jumped up . . . and sank back onto the catwalk.

That was when Lukos noticed it was quiet, but for the roar and crackle of the fire below. With his own footsteps silent, the sudden silence of the Hollow Men was glaring.

"Why didn't you jump?"

Lukos turned around. Any response he might have been thinking was replaced by fear. Three Avidum Hollows perched on or hanging from the catwalk, watched him, but it was the spectacled man that had frightened Lukos—the very same man he and Kit had seen fall over the railing not two minutes before. His right arm was limp, still useless, and his clothes were scorched. There were severe burn marks all over his face, which still held those thick, green, round glasses, now slightly cracked.

"You've run all this way," continued the man, non-plussed, "dodged our Hollows, dodged even us, and survived the streets as some innocent lamb with a common thief for a guide. Now you cannot muster the courage to jump out of that window?"

"How . . . how are you still alive?" Lukos was baffled.

The man inched toward Lukos. "To be honest, I'm disappointed. This is all very anti-climactic. I wanted more from you. Much more."

Lukos felt the rail against his back. The only way out of this was down, past the railing, through the window. He had to strike up the courage.

The man stepped closer, reaching out with his single good arm. He grabbed Lukos' collar before the young man had registered that he was so close.

"Mammon."

The man allowed a slight glance over his shoulder without releasing his hold on Lukos. "Mr. Zeb. I wasn't sure you would make it. How was dinner?"

Lukos watched as the man with the top hat—whom he had seen earlier at the Rusted Rose—strolled through the metallic tangle of Hollow Men. His eyes burned a dull orange, reflecting the hellish light from below. "I didn't get to finish. And I worked for that meal, too."

The spectacled man laughed, turning his gaze back to Lukos. "Always wanting more."

"Speak for yourself. What have you here, Mammon?"

"It's the boy."

"Yes, I see that. Let him go."

Mammon's clinch tightened around Lukos' collar as he spun to face Mr. Zeb, dragging Lukos around with him. "You cannot be serious! After everything that we've gone through to find him—"

"I can be serious, and indeed I am right now."

Lukos felt himself sailing through the air, given flight by some monstrous throw—and in the direction of the window. Terrified, and more than worried about the shards of glass jutting from the frame, Lukos flailed his left hand in front of him. He felt glass shatter against his metal hand as he flew through the window, the heat of the factory following him like a missile trail.

For a split second, he saw Kit on the ground below. Far below. He hoped she was not dead.

He hoped he was not about to die.

"Why, brother?" Mammon demanded, gritting teeth too white. Behind him, the Avidum Hollows began to inch forward, their small hands snapping open and closed in anticipation of a hunt.

Mr. Zeb held up a hand, straightening his shirt and jacket. "Calm yourself. We must wait a little longer." When a Hollow took another step forward, Mr. Zeb growled and the beast shrunk back.

"But it's time! All of the other pieces are in place except for locations."

"And to the others, this is true. But you and I," Mr. Zeb said, grabbing his fellow attendant by both shoulders, "we share larger desires. Greater needs. We require more time. If we are to have more power when we release Mr. Lucy, there are a few more things we must accomplish. But look at it this way . . . while we wait, we get to have a bit more fun."

Mammon sneered. "I don't give a damn about fun. Unlike you, my appetite is more than satisfied."

"You cannot tell me that more power and riches don't intrigue you?"

"For that, I will wait a little longer." A greedy twitch raised a corner of Mammon's mouth.

"Good. Now hear this. That girl guiding Lukos . . ."

"The thief?" Mammon raised a curious eyebrow. "What of her?"

"I've learned from Ash that the girl grew under the eye of Tom Vix. She is not the common urchin we thought her to be."

"Intriguing. What of it?"

"Think, Mammon, think. Where else will the girl lead Lukos, now that her only safe haven with Ash, is gone?"

"She's going to the Fox Den." Mammon's understanding grin grew with malice. "How long have we wanted to deal with that old fox?"

"Only too long. With Lukos off Limbo's streets, we can finally put LaCrucis back into commission."

"And the others? What do they think of this delay?"

Mr. Zeb waved a dismissing hand. "Bell Begor cares little of the time, so long as we succeed. Ash has grown soft. Mr. Levi is in no position to help or harm us. And of course, LaCrucis . . . well, there is not much left inside. You and I are the ones that stand to benefit the most from a little patience."

"You've been planning for something like this long before the boy's escape this morning, haven't you?"

"Do not accuse me of scheming, Mammon. The boy's abrupt change of heart was surely convenient. But I digress. You should go tend to yourself. You look like a mangled alley cat, and your suit is ruined."

This is pain, Lukos thought. *And it doesn't matter.* He had spent half of the day in moderate to severe pain, and he knew he could keep going. Lukos felt unstoppable. At least until he tried to stand.

A print was in the ground where his left arm had absorbed some of the impact, along with a small pool of blood from his previous wound. Lukos was sure that, without his metallic arm, he would have broken bones. He felt the open hole—it didn't bleed too much, but the bandages were loose.

Slowly, hurt arching from the balls of his feet all the way up to his shoulders, Lukos turned his head. Kit was a little ways from where he lay. A splotch of red running down from her hairline made him feel cold, alone. Another fire exploded from inside the building, and he hissed at her.

"Get up!"

She stirred, breathing becoming a little more than shallow, erratic, and he relaxed with the thought: *She's alive.* Lifting to his hands and knees, stopping briefly to gasp at the bruises already forming over his ribs, Lukos inched forward, grabbed hold of her shoulder, and gently shook.

"Kit, please, you have to get up. They're coming." *Why aren't they already here?*

Lukos cast a worried glance at the burning factory. Unlike the Rusted Rose, no one gathered or watched. He was worried Mammon or Mr. Zeb would walk out any second now.

Snippets of their strange conversation before they threw him out the window came back. While he was sure Mammon had every intention of taking him back to Lord Doyle, Mr. Zeb was harder to figure out. *What are they playing at?*

Kit's eyes fluttered open, glassy at first, and then clear, panicked. She jumped up, but immediately fell to the ground again, a pained grimace arresting her face.

"What is it?" Lukos asked.

"My leg," she whimpered. "I think it's broken." Some blood dripped into her eye, and she raised a shaky hand to her forehead.

Lukos wanted to lie down and stop this madness, but he knew the moment he gave in, it would be over, and not in the manner he wanted it to be. Instead, he picked Kit up and shoved himself away from the ground, ignoring as much as he could the creaking joints, stabbing pain, and dull aches as he stood.

"Put me down."

The complaint was weak, more of a whimper. Lukos ignored it, already stumbling into a swarm of shadows, away from the heat of the factory — and any eyes watching them.

"Hush. Which leg is it?"

"My right." She tried to move it, inhaling sharply. "I can walk, though."

"No."

She stopped arguing, but sighed in frustration. As she wrapped her arms around Lukos for better grip, he couldn't help feeling a surge of warmth.

"You've lost blood," he said, remembering her head wound.

"You more than me. I've survived worse. Listen, we need to go to . . . where did Biggy say . . . brickit, I can't believe they killed Biggy. Bastards," she whispered. Her eyes glistened, and her head fell onto his shoulder. "The Lake of Fire. We're going to go straight down this road and, and then left. No, right."

She went limp, and Lukos grunted at her dead weight, another jolt stabbing through his torso.

"Kit!"

"Concussion," she muttered. "I think."

"Don't you go to sleep. Tell me where to go and stay awake."

"Just . . . follow my lead."

They worked in tandem. Lukos listened to Kit's directions. It was a strange route through Industrial's filthy streets, and he wondered how much that route was hampered by her muddled state.

He also wondered at the worrying lack of Hollow Men chasing them, especially as slow as they were moving.

"Here," she said finally, facing a small footpath between buildings. Two black and dead trees withered over an equally sad bench. It sat too close to a water drain for it to be a comfortable resting place.

"Lift that grate up," she told him. He helped her to lean against the bench.

"The aqueducts again?"

"Yes."

"We must have passed one hundred drains tonight. Why the long walk to this one?"

She waved him off, steadying herself against the bench, which creaked noisily in complaint. Lukos shook his head but grasped the filthy bars with both hands. He pulled with all his might, surprised when the thick grate came up with little resistance.

"Some ways into the underground levels are safer than others," Kit explained. "There's less activity here, so this is one of them."

"Activity?"

"Hollows. The factory was another safe route down. Biggy was the lookout who guarded that entrance for the Fox Den, but . . ."

The thought of Biggy impaled on the Avidum's leg

flashed through Lukos's mind. He expected to feel that boiling anger again, but instead he felt emptiness. Both emotions terrified him. Beside him, Kit sniffled. "I should've known they would be there. Ash knew where I would go next. Stupid, so stupid!"

Lukos put a hand on her shoulder, and she fell into him, crying. He let her stay there for a moment, fighting his own guilt. He looked down into the hole, trying to stop remembering the images of death that had followed him all day.

The hole was dark, but some of the light from the street illuminated a small circle at the bottom. It was dry for a drainage system, but smelled rancid nonetheless. "There's no ladder."

"We'll have to jump down," Kit said, backing away from him. She wiped her eyes, a stone mask settling over her face.

He glanced at her leg, which was swollen beneath her dark leggings. "Let me go first. I'll catch you."

"You're as bad off as I am." She limped to the hole.

He put a hand out, holding her back. "Stop. You can

rely on me, you know."

Kit gave him a wary look, but nodded. Taking a final breath in the Industrial District's foul air, he jumped down into the even fouler air that would stay with them through the aqueducts. The jarring flash in his stomach took his breath away, worse than any of the other minor injuries tattooing his body. It was a moment before he stood at full height again.

"Ready," he called.

"Sh! Don't let your voice carry down there, even if this is one of the safer places." She appeared above the hole, limping slowly, careful of her injuries. She stood on one foot, hopped into the air, and down. Lukos caught her, struggling to stand from the sudden weight. She whimpered, a sound that wrenched at Lukos' gut and made him forget his own pain.

"What is it?"

"It's nothing," she lied, a hand frozen over her right leg. "I'll be fine. Let me down."

"I carried you this far. It's not like you're heavy or anything."

She shot him an angry glance — bright, indignant eyes giving him his answer. He put her down with strength and grace, and she hobbled along using the wall for support. Lukos gave up trying to help and followed her into the darkness. She stopped, body stiffening, which he mistook for pain.

"Kit, you don't have to walk, I can help —"

Kit's palm raised swift, silencing him. The silence stretching on, a plop from somewhere in the darkness caught Lukos' ear.

They plastered themselves against the wall, the greasy dirt evident against their skin. Lukos could hear his own heartbeat as they waited for whatever was in the darkness to pass . . . or to discover them. There was a large splash, and Lukos could see Kit's silhouette tremble.

Whatever it had been, the thing began to move away from them with intermittent splashes. They remained unmoving for a brief eternity until, wordless, Kit felt it safe to continue. Their movements became deliberate, careful not to make loud splashes with every step. A little farther, they were ankle deep in warm, murky water, every step a sloshing banshee crying to reveal their location.

"Careful here," Kit whispered, glancing at his stomach. "You don't want that to get infected."

Light filtered down from other drains on occasion, but it was rare and gave them as much comfort as it made them feel like targets in the ducts. Several tunnels merged, all seeming to flow toward the same epicenter, water steadily rising to their thighs.

Limbo was laden with drains. All of the water inside the copper walls — whether it be from human waste, use from the factories, or from the rare chance of acid rain — flowed down into the water cycling systems. Lukos wondered if that was where Kit was headed as they continued downward, only moving into the merging ducts to avoid those unseen sounds ahead or behind them. After dodging into another tunnel, Kit would find a way to venture downslope again.

"Are you ready?" Kit called over the now roaring water.

It was the first word either of them had spoken in hours. "Ready for what?" He recognized the sound of falling water and prayed to whatever fate was kind enough to listen that there would be no jumping into it.

She pulled him to the side of the tunnel, where he was relieved to see a ladder. He couldn't see where it ended, however.

"See you at the bottom," Kit told him, lowering herself toward the abyss. She muttered something to herself, wincing once or twice, and then slid down the sides of the ladder expertly. Lukos, not feeling as brave or fit for such tricks, took one rung at a time. After ten steps down, he was lost, clinging to a wall that was suspended in a seeming void of pitch above and below. The roar of the water several yards away only made the isolation seem greater.

Shoes slick, Lukos cried out as he slipped on a wet rung, bending one of the metal bars with his left hand as he regained footing. A chuckle from behind him made Lukos blush. He was holding onto the rungs for dear life . . . at the bottom of the ladder.

"You could have told me," he muttered.

She shrugged, and he thought he could see the hint of a grin in the shadows. "I was resting. We're almost there, but this is where it becomes dangerous. Stay close."

In a matter of minutes, they were wading through rushing waters, Lukos careful to keep his bandages above the foul water. They crawled out of one tunnel, against the flow, fighting their way upstream. An inhuman shriek from somewhere in the tunnels gave them speed.

"What is that?" he hissed, barely audible.

Kit didn't answer, but ducked into a new duct to their right. She flung an arm out, stopping Lukos from falling into a huge drain. Water gushed down before them, a warning of what could happen to them if they weren't mindful of their steps.

"It's this way," she told herself.

He followed her in silence once more as she navigated a complex system of tunnels, noting a hole here, a carving on the rock there. A skull hung from a low ceiling at one interval of drier tunnels. Lukos felt a tingling sensation between his shoulders, wondering what might be watching them from the dark.

Suddenly there was a huge gap in the brick tunnel wall. Kit and Lukos tumbled out of it, breathing air that smelled of fire and rock—an instant improvement from the horrid smell of the aqueducts.

It was the visual before them that truly amazed Lukos. He sucked in a deep breath, stumbling to his seat. His mind spun dizzy, the sight literally taking him off his feet.

Kit hobbled down a natural slope, hands reaching out to perspiring stalagmites. "The Lake of Fire. It's like nothing else, right?"

They had entered a huge cavern, nearly as large as all of Limbo itself, endless as far as their eyes could see, with heights challenging their perception. Stretching across the cavern was what looked like a lake — something Lukos had only ever seen in picture books and in paintings. Only this lake was topped with a tumultuous blaze. Gigantic pipes pumped to and from the Lake of Fire, their metal bodies blackened by the continual flames. Water poured from heights where aqueducts ended in mid air, or from other holes in the walls and ceilings.

"The cycling system," he said, struggling back to his feet. "So this is what it looks like. I can't believe all of this is down here."

Kit laughed. "This is just a small piece of the machine,

Lukos. The world under Limbo has no end. At least, none that we've found."

"And no end of dangers," said a new voice, quiet, but gruff. Lukos was aware of a knife suddenly positioned at an uncomfortable angle, with an equally uncomfortable pressure, in his back. Two soot-dirty and wet children walked around him, grabbing Kit by her shoulders and forcing her to stand.

"I taught you better," said the voice as the children secured Kit's arms and turned her around. "Too easy to sneak up on you."

Kit scowled at someone past Lukos' shoulder. "You didn't sneak up on me. I just didn't feel like saying hello."

"Doesn't surprise me, after the way you left. What are you doing here, Kit?"

"I need to get out of Limbo."

"No."

Kit's expression remained the same, but Lukos could detect stress, maybe panic, in her voice. "You didn't even hear me out."

"Don't need to. I know why you came. Heard you got

yourself in trouble with the Hollows, and with Ash. With her gone, you have no haven, nowhere to hide. Am I right so far?"

She nodded, the children on both sides of her snickering.

"And so you come crawling back to me, like the arrogant girl that you are, expecting that I would take pity on you. I wondered if you would come to me for help . . . just didn't think you would actually have the gall."

"I will die up there," said Kit. Her weighted words stopped the man's easy, bitter flow, if only for a second.

"Well," he said after a moment, "you gave up the Den's protection when you left. You're choice, I'll have you remember."

Lukos felt the knife drop, a strong hand grabbing his shoulder and turning him around. He was able to put a face to the overwhelming musty smell emanating from the individual holding him hostage. The man was just beginning to show his age, streaks of white spattering his red flyaway hair. A look of surprise hung on the man's sharp features, and whatever else he was about to say seemed to be stuck on his tongue. He leaned back, gripping his metal cane tight. Lukos' vision swam for a moment, distorting the man's face.

"You. What is your name, boy?" the man demanded, squeezing his shoulder.

"Lukos," he answered dumbly, blinking away the fuzziness.

The man squinted, and his hand slid away as he staggered backward. "Lukos. Last name?"

"I don't know."

"You don't . . . right. Well . . . All the ruckus up top makes sense now." The man ran a hand through his hair and over the stubble on his chin. "David, Star, let go of Kit. She can't do anything to us. No more than before, at least."

The two children released Kit, letting a pout escape their lips before each gave her a hug. They took their place beside their leader once more.

"Fine," he said, leaning on his cane. "I've changed my mind."

"Just like that?" Kit asked, eyes narrowed. She glanced

at Lukos, calculating, analyzing, but saying nothing more.

"I can change it again, if it'd please you. Don't press your luck. The Den is about to make its next stop, and it looks like you both are injured. You could use some medical attention."

Kit threw a hand up. "Sure. That would be nice."

As the man and two children started to walk, Lukos turned to Kit. "Is this what we traveled all the way down here for? A grumpy old man and some kids?"

Kit sighed. "Something like that. Lukos, meet Mr. Tom."

"Tom Vix," the man called over his shoulder. "Pleasure's mine, Lukos. Just be careful around this old man and his kids."

Mr. Tom apparently had excellent hearing. Lukos would have blushed, had he not already lost so much blood. He ducked in line with Kit as she limped forward. They passed through a small forest of stalagmites and over a rock ridge, finally revealing their destination. Lukos gave a woozy smile at what lay hidden beyond. What could only be described as a small village of children, was setting up beds, tents, crates of food, and barrels of water. And that was when he truly felt relief.

"We did it," he told Kit. "We escaped Limbo."

She sighed and shook her head. "No. We haven't. Not yet."

Mr. Tom appeared at Lukos' shoulder. "You're both in for a tough time of it." He leaned down, whispering to Lukos only, "And happy birthday, by the way. It's your birthday today, isn't it?"

Lukos stared at him in shock, barely registering Kit's concerned and questioning glances between him and the old vagabond.

Mr. Tom chuckled, patting them both on their shoulders, and moved ahead to his camp. He turned back once before heading off to help set up, yelling at them in his signature gruff tone: "Welcome to the Fox Den!"

The attendants sat or stood assembled in the Oudemonium as Limbo's archduke stewed in his chair. Mr. Zeb,

Mammon, Bell Begor, and Ash were in different stages of disrepair, bandages, and — in Ash's case — furious wallowing, all listening to O'Toole try to comprehend the tale he had just heard.

"Help me understand this correctly. You and Mammon both saw Lukos, had him cornered in a factory. He jumps out of a window and escapes you completely. Is that right?" Shekelton O'Toole did not open his eyes, his fingers steepling over the bridge of his nose.

Mr. Zeb nodded lavishly, playing with a fly that buzzed before him. "Accurate enough, my lord. There was of course, a fire to contend with. By the time we entered the street, both he and the girl were gone."

"The second fire last night." Ash glared at Mr. Zeb.

O'Toole continued. "You're all fireproof! So two human children outrun you both, withstanding falls from a third story window. Meanwhile you, what, take the stairs?"

"We do take injuries too, you know." Mr. Zeb pretended to be flustered, gesturing to Mammon in the seat next to him, who was wrapped in several bandages, his arm in a sling. Mammon grunted. Next to him sat Begor, who still had shards of glass sticking out from her face.

"I don't care!" O'Toole was standing now, slamming a fist into his desk. "You do the job I gave you, no matter the cost!" He sat back down. "Where are they now?"

And at this, Mr. Zeb shared a look with Mammon, smiling his most devilish smile. "The Second Circle, my lord. They've gone underground to take refuge with Tom Vix."

Shekelton O'Toole leaned back in his chair, the giant gears outside the room providing a constant, grinding rumble that filled the silence. "Vix. That traitor."

"I could release him, my lord. LaCrucis . . ."

O'Toole's eyes snapped open, giving Mr. Zeb a hard look.

"Lukos and this girl are underground," the attendant explained. "Your precious townspeople will not need be worried of LaCrucis, never know of him. And while he is awake, Tom Vix will be . . . tended to . . . as well. Kill two birds with one stone—one horrible, effective stone."

"This was what you were after all along, isn't it?" asked O'Toole. "To wake that forsaken monster and set him loose again."

"My lord, of course not."

"Do not lie to me!"

A flash of irritation passed over Mr. Zeb's face, and he caught the fly he'd been playing with mid-air, crushing it. Mammon stiffened, watching both master and servant.

"I cannot lie to you," countered Mr. Zeb.

O'Toole held out his hand, displaying his silver ring. "Prove it, then."

Mr. Zeb looked at the ring with distaste, but leaned forward in his chair. He grabbed O'Toole's hand, the silver making contact immediately.

"I swear to you, Shekelton O'Toole, my master, I set out with no intention of raising LaCrucis from his rest."

He pulled away, but O'Toole held his hand there for a moment, another moment still, before letting go. Smoke wafted between them as Mr. Zeb displayed the blistered skin where he'd come in contact with the silver.

"See?" he said. "No lies."

O'Toole grunted, and waved his hand at the two attendants. "Do what you will, so long as the boy comes to me alive."

Mr. Zeb and Mammon stood, bowing slightly. They left him to his papers and reports, exiting for the elevator. Ash and Begor remained, as O'Toole required their reports of the previous nights' findings.

"How did you do that?" asked Mammon in the elevator cab. "How did you lie to him just now?"

"We aren't mere underlings, Mammon. We never have been, and I don't intend on becoming one now."

The elevator descended with a whine and squeal, passing the first floor of the Oudemonium, plummeting through the floor. All became dark, until they were descending through the middle of a spiral staircase of inhuman proportions. A burning lake was visible in the distance, as well as more otherworldly sights.

The small car continued to plummet through thick layers of earth into another cavern, this one much quieter, darker, and colder than before, full of slush. They continued to descend, passing another layer of earth and emerging in a place that glittered with many variations of minerals and splendid stones, patches of the cavern emptied of its valuable materials. Automatons mined the cavern endlessly, falling out of sight as the elevator descended one more level. It began to slow, coming to a smooth halt at a metal platform. This cavern was also cold, a black river running underneath the landing, chilling the surface.

"After you, Mammon."

The two attendants walked over a metal bridge to where large, frigid pods stood like giant insect eggs.

"And now, the games begin," said Mr. Zeb, sliding the door of the first pod open. "Wake up, my brother. Listen to me . . . Tom Vix, and Lukos Lyall. You remember these names? Does your blind rage ignite at their very mention?"

Two wide eyes slowly flickered open in the pod — two shining pearls in an inky sea of shadowed features. The thing inside growled, wrathful, and a pale, lean hand shot forward, grabbing the lapel of Zeb's suit. The attendant grinned, patting the hand with a strange affection.

"Wake, LaCrucis."

About The Author

C. Michael McGannon was born in Mannheim, Germany while his parents were serving abroad. As soon as his hand figured out what to do with a pencil, he was drawing wild monsters and eerily recognizable stick figures of his family, and as soon as he could string words together on paper, well . . . he's been crafting stories ever since.

He loves dragons, foxes, and sushi, and is a connoisseur of a well-timed, *the-cheesier-the-better pun*. His free time is spent enjoying family and friends, gaming, and engaged in the deep study of folklore and mythology from around the world. As much as possible, Michael enjoys traveling to fan conventions, meeting readers face to face, and sharing adventures from his own love of storytelling.

McGannon is the co-author of the best-selling fantasy series for young adults, *Charlie Sullivan and the Monster Hunt-*

ers (Wyvern's Peak Publishing); a collection of dark fiction stories for adults, *KAOS Obsidere: The Nightmare Has Begun (Dark Waters Press)*; and a collection of original stories about Japanese yokai titled, *Yokai Tales: Stories From Japan's Grand and Mysterious Traditions of Folklore (Redcap Studios)*, in addition to the *Hollow World* series.

He is also co-host of The Monster Guys Podcast, the Yokai Podcast, and Faerie Tales Podcast—weekly conversations exploring interests in folklore, mythology, and storytelling from countries and tribes the world over.